"If you are looking for a new and exciting read that will leave you wanting to attempt to talk to your refrigerator or chuckle to yourself, this book is it!"

—Rebekah Engleright, educator at Messalonskee Middle

SECOND CHANCES

SECOND CHANCES

— A Toki Tooley Mystery Series —

Amelia Kronser-Cole

Published by
RHYOLITE PRESS LLC
Colorado Springs, Colorado

Published in the United States of America
by Rhyolite Press LLC
P.O. Box 60144
Colorado Springs, Colorado 80960
www.rhyolitepress.com

Second Chances
Kronser-Cole, Amelia

August 15, 2020

Library of Congress Control Number: 2020913540
ISBN# 978-1-943829-12-5

Publisher's Cataloging-in-Publication Data

Names: Kronser-Cole, Amelia, author.
Title: Second chances : a Toki Tooley mystery series / Amelia Kronser-Cole.
Description: Colorado Springs, CO: Rhyolite Press, 2020.
Identifiers: LCCN: 2020913540 | ISBN: 978-1-943829-12-5
Subjects: LCSH Psychics--Fiction. | High school students--Fiction. | Colorado--Fiction. | Family--Fiction. | Detective and mystery stories. | BISAC YOUNG ADULT FICTION / Mysteries & Detective Stories | YOUNG ADULT FICTION / Paranormal, Occult & Supernatural
Classification: LCC PZ7.1.K7855 Sec 2020 | DDC [Fic]--dc23

PRINTED IN THE UNITED STATES OF AMERICA

Cover design, book design/layout by Suzanne Schorsch and Donald Kallaus

For Emi, Elaine, Mom, and Elliott,
the women of the past, present, and future.

TABLE OF CONTENTS

CHAPTER:

One: Warnings   1

Two: The Journal   9

Three: The New Kid   19

Four: Best Buzzer   31

Five: Breaking and Entering   41

Six: Mardi Paws   51

Seven: The Crime Scene   61

Eight: Rankin   67

Nine: The Protector   79

Ten: Wrong   89

Eleven: Grandmother Emi   111

Twelve: Suspicions   121

Thirteen: The Blue Truck   131

Fourteen: Liam   141

Fifteen: Déjà Vu   157

My name is Toki Tooley. Yes, that's really my name. Please don't laugh for too long. I've got to tell you this secret. You seem like a pretty trustworthy person, so listen up.

I talk to the spirits of the world, and they talk back to me. Everything in my life was fine until I moved to the town of Devil's Ford in Colorado. Now, I have the pressure of fitting in to a new school, surviving the students who are stuck at the lunch detention table for life, and solving the murder of Liam Paxton, a local high school senior who was found dead in the middle of a snowy night.

If that wasn't bad enough, there's this mysterious "Dark Spirit" that will consume the whole town if I don't solve the murder in time.

Think it sounds complicated? Welcome to my life.

Chapter One: Warnings

Wednesday, February 3rd. 8:03 p.m.

I DIDN'T SEE the Paxton kid when he was killed.

I felt it.

Or, more specifically, I felt *something* when I had gone outside that night. There was a thick snow falling. The wind was icy. It blew the heavy flakes of snow around like a whirlwind, going this way and that way. It was a storm unlike any I had ever seen before. Living on the Oregon coast my whole life, I had felt cold, and I had seen snow—but I had experienced nothing like this. The granite-flecked, footstool-sized boulder that I had been eyeing since the move already had a blanket of white covering it.

It was officially a blizzard, and it blew my mind. I thought I knew everything there was to know about snowstorms. They seemed pretty easy to picture, anyway. As a little kid at school, I remember watching some musical about a group named the Donner party that traveled the Oregon trail. They got stuck in a blizzard in the Sierra Nevada Mountains on the way to California. Spoiler alert: it didn't end well for most of them. It also didn't end well for the little kids watching the musical. When your catchiest song is called, "Cannibal is Just Another Word for Survival," your target audience is probably

1

not a group of seven-year olds. By the time the play was over, most of the kids in the auditorium were sobbing and freaking out about man-eating "cannon balls." This is just an educated guess, but I'm pretty sure whoever booked that traveling theater group had a lot of explaining to do the next day.

Being in a blizzard in the Colorado Rockies, however, was way different than watching a community theater production of one. Paper confetti and a fog machine had nothing on Mother Nature. As I looked out the window, I was amazed at how little I could see. Whenever the wind would blow the right way, the tree line just beyond our backyard would completely disappear. I suddenly had a new appreciation for how that Donner party could have gotten so hopelessly lost just by walking.

My parents were gone that night, off to see a movie about people driving fast cars, beating up bad guys and escaping explosions in slow motion. That sounded about as appealing to me as a lobotomy, so I decided to stay home and visit the boulder in the back. I had been dying the whole time to see it, but I had to do it alone. I didn't want my dad's worried looks and threats about therapy to interrupt our time together.

My new winter jacket swallowed me as I walked carefully from the back porch to the end of our yard. The wind had died down so now there was a kinder snow falling. It looked like the inside of some cheesy little snow globe. I shivered, completely unaware that a new meaning of the word "cold" was awaiting me in this little town of Devil's Ford.

I trudged through the thick piles of snow and reached the big rock at the border of our backyard. Excitement pumped through my heart. It wasn't just my own excitement; I could feel the air buzzing around me as I approached.

I used a puffy sleeve to wipe away the thick layer of snow that topped the rock. Digging into my pocket, I pulled out a small red carnation I had bought from a gas station earlier that day.

"Hi," I said. "I guess you're pretty used to this weather by now. I'm not."

I gently placed the flower on top of the rock.

"I hope you like this. I had to buy it at a Stop-and-Spend down the road. We just moved here." I looked around the world of white surrounding me. "I don't think I'm going to be growing my own flowers anytime soon."

Removing one of my gloves, I put my hand on top of the rock and closed my eyes. It was so cold that for a moment, I thought about coming back on a different day. I would have a lot of explaining to do if my parents found me frozen to a rock in the backyard. Luckily for me a reply came pretty quickly.

New? The rock chirped.

I nodded. It seemed like I was right about this rock—it was ready to talk to someone.

"Yeah, I just moved here from Oregon. Pretty far away. I've never been to Colorado before."

I kept my hand on the granite face for a moment longer. It warmed slightly. Some time passed—it was comforting just to sit in the presence of a friendly spirit again. It made me feel like I was home. After awhile, I stood up.

"I'll come visit tomorrow," I promised. I knew not to push my luck—once an object had spoken, a few words at most, it needed some time to process its next thought.

I had turned and was heading back inside when I felt *it*. I gasped and fell to the ground. Something had cut the breath from my lungs. I could feel a deep dread snaking around my arms and legs, almost seeming to tie me to the ground. My mind was filled with a crashing, twisting noise and a scream of pain. In desperation, I reached out and threw my hand on the ground.

"What is it?" I asked through gritting teeth. A metallic taste filled my mouth as soon as I asked the question.

Even though every sense was overwhelmed, I clearly heard the cry from the frozen layer of dirt below my trembling fingers.

Gone. Gone.

I DON'T REMEMBER exactly when I started talking to the spirits in the world, but I do remember when they started talking back to me. Thanking different objects around the world was something I had learned from my Japanese mom. She was pretty Westernized about most things, but the tradition of respecting and valuing objects stuck with her and got passed to me. We thanked the flowers when we passed them in the garden. We said hello to the car in the morning. We greeted our little house on the coast every day when we got home.

One day, when I was three, my mother and I went for a walk on the coast. It was a typical Oregon day. The gray sky stretched across the churning ocean. The waves washed up all sorts of interesting things on the rocky, cold beach. My mom had brought a bag with her and was picking up trash. That was her coping method when she had a bad day at work. I toddled after her as usual, cheerfully addressing anything I saw.

A giant, stately piece of driftwood sat on the beach. It looked like it had been there for ages. I grinned, ran over to it, and dug into my pocket. Pulling out a few soggy pieces of Cheerios, I put them in one of the swirling knots as an offering, saying hello and running my hand over the sea-worn wood.

Greetings, the driftwood replied in a dignified voice.

Most mothers would have chalked it up to an overactive imagination if their three-year-old had told them that a piece of wood had just talked back to them, but my mother just smiled at me.

"Your Grandmother Emi used to say that's the spirits talking back," she told me, bending down to grab my chubby little hands. "That's quite the honor, Toki. Only the bravest people listen and hear what they have to say."

Then she got that far-away, dark look in her eyes. It was the same look she got whenever she talked about her mother. I had never met Grandmother Emi. We lived our quiet lives in Oregon, and all I knew was that she was far away in some mountain town in Colorado. Every year my brother Ken and I would get a birthday card from her, but the same message was always scrawled in neat letters.

Happy Birthday, cherished one.
May the spirits be kind and gentle to you.

Admittedly, Ken and I would always turn her card upside-down, trying to shake out some cash or a check, but nothing ever accompanied the birthday cards. Just the same message, every year.

By myself, I learned how to talk to the spirits quickly. It didn't seem strange; I was young and probably kind of dense. I thought everyone knew the same rules that I did. Some spirits were ready and willing to talk, like the toys at a shop or a crowd of daffodils on a summer day. Others could be coaxed into conversation with an offering. Food worked well. Plants always appreciated water. Some spirits enjoyed being pampered—a little dusting or removing years' old grime. I learned to carry a little tool bag with me to barter or bribe the more stubborn ones. Some spirits, on the other hand, refused to talk. They were too angry, too proud, or just not interested in a conversation with a preschooler.

Those spirits who did talk usually said one word a day. The really talkative ones went up to three, but there were never full sentences, just enough to communicate a thought or a feeling. You could also tell the personality of an object based on a conversation with it. The piece of driftwood on the beach was always a gentleman. Pool toys were fun loving, but never had anything earth-shattering to say. The mascara at the drugstore always thought it was better than anyone else and required a lot of pampering before insulting you. Stubborn, bold, timid, adventurous, loving, distant—I talked to them all.

My older brother was never quite on the same level with the spirits as I was. Part of me suspects he sometimes heard them, but Ken was too athletic, too popular, and honestly too normal to really listen to the spirits around him. My dad also spoke his own language, but only to his best friends.

"A dog's bark," my dad would tell me, "can tell you a lot of things, Toki. You just have to listen."

I was amazed that every time a dog barked, whined, or growled at my dad, he truly seemed to understand it. Hungry, sometimes. Bored. Frightened. Whatever the dog wanted, my dad could decode it. To my young mind, it all made sense. Mom and I could talk to the spirits, Dad could talk to dogs, and Ken was the only one who could actually effectively talk to people.

In case you haven't noticed, yeah. We were a weird little family.

School was finally the place that taught me exactly how different I was from everyone else. It all happened on the first day in kindergarten when a boy used safety scissors to crudely carve a triangle into the desk. He smiled at me, presenting his finished masterpiece.

"Look, I made a square!" he announced.

Hand on the desk, I listened and frowned.

"The desk says 'ouch,'" I informed him primly. "You shouldn't hurt it anymore. Also, that's a triangle, not a square."

He stopped creating his carvings that day, fortunately. Unfortunately, he spent the rest of the year pelting me with broken crayons when the teacher wasn't looking. While the desk thanked me profusely, I spent the rest of kindergarten pulling Crayola shavings out of my hair. I learned a lesson that day that stuck with me for the next eleven years—most people weren't interested in what the spirits had to say, and I was even less interested in what most people had to say.

As you can imagine, when my parents announced we were moving to Colorado, there weren't any lifelong friends that I sobbed over leaving behind. I was probably the only person alive that got teary saying goodbye to driftwood.

There was something bothering me about the whole moving situation. I didn't want to argue with my parents, but when they had announced that we were leaving Oregon for the town of Devil's Ford, Colorado, there wasn't any discussion. Grandmother Emi was in very bad shape, my mother stiffly told me. Her memory was getting worse. It was doubtful she could care for herself anymore. There was no one else to rely on, and she desperately needed her family.

"Maybe she should've visited us when she had the chance. I've never even met her," I had pointed out at the time. Dad kinda looked like he agreed with me, but he knew better than to argue with my mom when she was all stressed out. Not me. I loved kicking the hornets' nest every now and then.

That familiar We're-Talking-About-Grandmother-Emi-and-I'd-Rather-Eat-Angry-Wasps look darkened my mother's face as she replied, "Toki, as much as she may have wanted to visit, she couldn't. She's a very busy woman. She has been her whole life. Now she needs us, and we need to go."

That was that. We packed up all our things, said goodbye to Ken (a freshman at the University of Oregon and probably very relieved that his bizarre family wasn't going to be visiting him at college), and moved into town right in time to experience the mother of all snowstorms.

It may have been the spirits trying to give us a giant warning, but we were all oblivious to it. With the move, the unpacking, all of the new places and objects to explore, we were distracted and tired. After the ground screamed at me, I knew something was wrong in Devil's Ford. It was an impossible sign to miss.

After I pulled myself off the ground that night, I dragged myself into the house, thinking about the earth's words. *Gone, gone.* The words bounced around my head, loudly filling every corner. There were still feelings of darkness like pinpricks all over my body. I had to admit the spirits in Devil's Ford spoke a lot louder than the ones in Oregon. There had never been any spirit this distressed before. I shivered even as I sat under a blanket by the roaring fireplace.

This wasn't just a warning. It was a cry for help.

Chapter Two: The Journal

Sunday, February 7th. 4:29 p.m.

THE CONSTANT TICKING of the clock on my grandmother's bedside table was the loudest noise in the room. Every second passing seemed to sound louder and louder. My head throbbed in response, and my thoughts went from annoyed to downright homicidal. If I didn't have such a deep appreciation for the spirit of all objects, I would've certainly smashed that particular clock against the white brick walls of the nursing home.

The clock obviously wanted me to talk to it. I wasn't in the mood.

"Pipe down," I hissed at it.

It only ticked louder in response. Sometimes really stubborn spirits will act this way, doing anything to get your attention. Normal people might think that their house is haunted by an evil presence, but trust me, it's usually just an old floorboard trying to tell you that it would like a nice mopping every now and then.

I shifted. My heavy winter jacket scraped against the plastic chair. My hand crept toward the pocket where I knew my cell phone was resting. I was so tempted to take it out to research more places to visit in Colorado. I knew that there were so many parks and national forests just waiting to be explored and talked to. It would help pass the time, anyway, instead of just sitting and counting the number of bricks in the opposite wall.

Just as I pulled the cell phone out, I heard a hum, usually a clue that a spirit was trying to get my attention. I looked up at a hand-printed sign opposite me, politely reminding me to keep all cell phones and electronics off during visiting hours. I didn't need to talk to the sign's spirit to know what it was trying to tell me. *Follow rules!*

I rolled my eyes. Did sitting here alone with a comatose grandmother even qualify as visiting? My parents were filling out paperwork in the hospital administration office. I wished they would hurry back so that we could leave. Yeah right. Hoping for those two to do anything with a sense of urgency was as useless as hoping a snowball would melt in a freezer.

Which, thinking on it, was an appropriate comparison considering the state of this room. It was freezing. Admittedly, ever since my strange night in the backyard, I was always cold. It seemed impossible to get warm, even though I piled layers and layers of clothes on. It was like cold had seeped in my bones and infected them from the inside. My dad said the chill was because of the river running through town, but I had my doubts. Nobody else seemed to ever be as cold as I was.

This room, however, was like an icebox. The thermostat only said 62, which I felt was a crime. The assisted living home must have decided to cut corners on the heating. My sleeping grandmother only had a thin blue blanket covering her. It didn't seem like nearly enough to protect a fragile old lady from the frigid chill in the air. I was stuck in this room until my parents returned; at least I could make sure grandmother didn't freeze to death.

I popped my head out the door leading into the corridor, looking for a nurse or attendant or even (fingers crossed!) my parents, but there was no one except for a grizzled-face man with blonde, thinning hair sitting in a plastic chair a few doors down. He had his hands wrapped around a paper cup of coffee and looked up expectantly when the door opened. When he saw me, his eyes dropped again.

Well, no help there. Back in the room I began searching, my clunky boots squeaking against the floor. The clock was still ticking loudly, insisting that I talk to it. I pointedly ignored it—really, some spirits must learn patience somehow. I began searching the cupboards in the room. Finally, at the tip-top of one, I found an identical thin blue blanket. Two useless blankets were better than one, I reasoned to myself. I gently layered it on top of Grandmother Emi's frail body, smoothing out the wrinkles.

The clock on the night stand now had a rattle when it ticked, a sign that it wouldn't wait nicely for conversation any longer. I sighed and moved to the bedside, finally taking the impatient spirit in my hands. It looked like an old-fashioned clock, the kind that you would put on a mantle, though this one had been sitting on a black book on the night stand. The clock was rectangular, about the size of a toaster. Stained with a deep-colored oak hue, it had simple metal numbers and pointy hands. I only had to hold it for a moment before it spoke.

Important.

"I'm sure you think you are," I responded. It was always the same way with antiques, always thinking they were more expensive than they actually were. That was the sole reason I avoided second-hand stores. Whenever I ventured into one, almost all of the items demanded that I take them to be valued on *Antiques Roadshow*, and a lot of those spirits had a hard time accepting "no" for an answer. Some of them would even fly off the shelf and break themselves in order to get their way. Imagine trying to explain that over and over to a store clerk. If I didn't go out of my way to stay away from the thrift stores, I'd probably be banned from them anyway.

As I placed the clock back on the night stand, I had the eerie feeling I was being watched. I turned. There was Grandmother Emi, sitting straight up in bed, staring at me with a questioning look. Her dark eyes were worried, almost panicked. She reached out a hand and grabbed my wrist with the intensity of a snapping turtle.

"What... day?" She croaked, fingers tightening.

I suppressed every neuron in my brain that was firing for me to scream. If this nursing home was against the quiet beeping of electronics, I couldn't imagine they'd look too kindly on outright screaming in terror.

"It's February 7th," I whispered, thankful I had gone to the bathroom before visiting. That would be my luck to make a great first impression by soiling myself.

Her eyes darted back and forth as if she were desperately trying to recall something. She looked over at the clock on her bedside, placing her hand on the top of it for a moment. To my relief, she released my wrist and pushed herself up on shaky, skinny elbows. I watched her pull the black book from under the clock and flip open its pages. It was an old book, the cover cracked and peeling. She stopped on a page and pulled a pen from the back cover. She began scribbling so furiously that I thought her fingers were going to fly off.

"I should go and get the nurse," I stammered, gently easing myself away. Yeah right, a nurse. A better option would be a tranquilizer dart gun.

I should have learned my lesson. You don't do anything around Grandmother Emi slowly.

With a speed and ferocity I've never before witnessed in a senior citizen, Grandmother reached to one side of her bed and brandished a cane. She whipped the hooked end around to corral me and pulled me back toward the bed like she had reeled in a catch.

"No time," she said tersely. "Before I forget again, you must..." her eyes looked up at me carefully. For a moment, she stopped, voice softening. "Toki. Grandchild. I know you hear the spirits. You must be very brave, indeed."

That was debatable, especially considering that this 65-year-old woman had almost made me wet myself.

I swallowed. "I... don't know. They speak, and I listen. That's not really brave."

Her eyes twinkled. "It takes more courage than you think to listen to others. That's why you must be the one, Toki. You must save them."

She held the book in her hands, closing her eyes. I marveled for a moment. I knew exactly what she was doing; she was talking to it, just like I talked to the spirits. To see someone else do it, though, was strange and wonderfully familiar. It made me feel like someone maybe could finally understand me.

"I may lose myself again. It's been happening more. No warnings. Time is running out for them." She opened her eyes, carefully placing the book in my hands. "What I know is in that journal. The rest, you must find. Speak to it, Toki, and it will guide you."

She watched me expectantly. I did what I knew best. I placed my hand on the journal and listened. I was shocked by what I heard next.

Welcome, Protector-in-training Toki. It is your time to save them.

A strange white light began glowing from the journal. It snaked out from the cover, wrapping around my wrists like a pair of handcuffs and quickly traveling up my arms. The white light grew brighter, covering over my eyes like a thick fog. It was getting harder to breathe. The last thing I remember were my grandmother's mournful words.

"Good luck Toki. For what it is worth, I am sorry."

"So," MY MOTHER ventured in a hopeful voice, once we were back in our family car, "how was your visit with Grandmother Emi?"

'Baffling' was what I wanted to scream. 'Creepy. Mind-numbing'. I found myself instead answering, "Wonderful, thank you" which sounded as about convincing as I felt.

When I had come to my senses after the white haze, I was sitting back in the chair as if nothing had ever happened. Grandmother was snoozing obliviously under her blankets, looking all fragile and innocent again. For a moment I was sure I was going crazy. This had to be the onset of some horrible, delusional disease. I had heard about people going crazy up in the high altitudes of Everest—mountain sickness, they called it. Maybe moving up to Devil's Ford in the Rockies was going to be the thing that broke me. It wouldn't be long now until someone found me gnawing on my own leg bone like one of those Donner folks.

I wasn't going crazy, though. Before I left the room, I noticed two things.

One, the annoying clock on the mantel was gone.

Two, and most unsettling, the journal was in the pocket of my jacket.

It was taking me a moment to process my thoughts. The journal had spoken back. That within itself was normal enough; spirits in different objects spoke to me every day. The thing that I was having a hard time wrapping my mind around was how much it had said. Three words—that was the most I had ever heard a spirit say before and it was usually only the really talkative ones at that. This one had said two complete sentences with the perfection of an English professor. It had also known my name. The rules about spirits that I had thought I pinned down before were unraveling, and it made me nervous. What else was out there that I didn't know?

In the front seat, my dad and my mom shared a look with each other that didn't go unnoticed by me. My silence must have spoke volumes. Dad cleared his throat.

"Your first day of school is tomorrow!" he announced lamely as if any of us had forgotten that. "Are you nervous?"

I shrugged. Not so much nervous as reluctant. The spirits, well, I completely understood them. My own classmates—I'd rather hang out with a spatula all day. It'd have far more interesting things to say.

My dad adjusted his rear-view mirror. "You know, Toki, your mother and I were just talking, and we were thinking…"

Oh boy. This was going to be interesting. I saw Mom raise her eyebrows at him and look away, sighing.

"Well *I* was thinking," he continued, "it's a brand-new start for all of us, you know? Maybe some things should change now that we've all matured a little."

He waited for me to say something, but I refused. I knew what he was going to say; he had only brought it up a million times before. I wasn't going to feed into it. If he wanted to say it, he could do all the hard work himself.

"Maybe it's time we leave the 'spirit talk' behind us," he said quickly. "I know that kids at your last school, well, they gave you hell about it. Teased you and everything. Maybe if you just stopped whatever it is you do, you could try to be…"

"Normal?" I asked quietly.

Dad groaned as Mom threw him a murderous look.

"Toki, if you try to find normal, you'll be searching your whole life," she said, turning around and facing me with her kind eyes. "I think what your father is trying, rather poorly, to say is that with a new start comes new opportunity. No one would ever suggest you stop talking to the spirits, but maybe you could be more discreet. After all, does anybody really need to know what a plunger is thinking?"

She had a point. Trying to explain the innermost thoughts of the household plunger hadn't exactly won me any friends in Oregon. It did, however, win my parents a rather awkward visit to the school psychologist.

"Things will go to a new normal faster than you think," my dad assured me. "I just want your normal to be something you're happy with, that's all."

If I hadn't had my head wrapped around the puzzle of the white light in Grandmother Emi's room, I might have laughed out loud at that. Normal? My life had always been anything but normal, and the events of the past hour proved that nothing, not even a move halfway across the country, would ever change that.

LATER THAT NIGHT, I sat in my room and pulled the journal from my pocket. It was the first time I acknowledged it since Grandmother had given it to me.

I put my hand on the cover and listened.

Rule one, it stated immediately as if it had been waiting for me to return, *the clock is both your enemy and your friend.*

"That makes no sense," I told it quietly, not wanting my parents to hear that I was throwing their sage advice out the window mere hours after they had so graciously imparted it to me.

Rule two: their future is not your future. Rule three: Write the name but be certain—there is no going back. Rule four: Only those who approach the light will remember. Rule five: Second chances only are given to all who accept them. Please sign your name with an acceptance or denial on the last page once you are ready to become a true Protector.

Just like that, it stopped. I gritted my teeth, placing my hand on the journal again, but nothing happened.

"Great. Really instructive. You would think you could be a little more forthcoming with how talkative you are."

Getting nowhere with conversation, I decided to open it to read what Grandmother had written. A business card fluttered out and fell to the ground. It didn't have a name, but there was a hastily scrawled phone number in long, sloppy handwriting. I tossed the business card aside, uninterested.

The inside pages were covered with the neat handwriting I recognized from her yearly birthday cards to Ken and me. There was an unfathomable number of dates, places, names—some were crossed out, others checked. There were question marks over every page and maps—rough sketches of rooms and buildings. At the end of almost every entry, there was a strange, iridescent circle on the page. It almost looked like it had been embossed with some shimmering ink. Three of the entries, however, had a dark red stamp. The last entry didn't have a circle—just a few lines written under the date.

> 2. 03
> D: L. Paxton (17) STU - CHS
> C.S. 1800 Delta Rd., f. 8:33 P.M.
> H & R ???
> TT nr bdy
> Blnt f. Trma
> Phone???

Grandmother Emi had said what she knew was in the journal. The journal had given me a set of rules. I had a boatload of information but had absolutely no idea what to do with it or even what it all meant. My hand lingered on my pillow.

Sleep? It asked gently.

Good suggestion. That was the only thing said to me today that made sense.

Chapter Three: The New Kid

Monday, February 8th. 7:35 a.m.

MOM WAVED CHEERFULLY (for a really, really long time) as I slunk from the car door and began the trek toward my new high school. Chamberlain High School was the only high school in town. As embarrassing as it was to have my mom waving at me like a hoard of gnats was attacking her, I also felt completely alone. My dad had given me a cheerful thumbs-up and wink before I left the house which I took as a sign to remember our "talk" from yesterday. Nothing would have felt more comforting than to listen to the spirits right now, but I at least half-heartedly told my dad I would try to talk to humans first. That morning in front of a mirror, I had even practiced, "Hey, hello, hi, how's it going?" I felt like I was magically becoming lamer and lamer with each passing second.

Be yourself? The mirror suggested.

I made a face at it. Easy for you to say. You don't have to worry about three-second first impressions.

It turned out all my anxiety was for nothing. The moment I entered the main office to get my schedule, I was immediately pounced upon by Mrs. Fieldman. She was single-handedly the most enthusiastic assistant principal I'd ever met. Turned out, this school had locked down a plan for new students. The problem was everybody at Chamberlain High School had grown up in Devil's Ford. New kids were even more rare than snow days; every day was a snow day in Devil's Ford, and from what I heard, school was never cancelled. When the office staff learned they were finally getting a new student, they were beside themselves. I was going to be the first official student to complete their New Student Orientation.

The word "guinea pig" came to mind as I sat in Mrs. Fieldman's office as she pounded my information into her computer with unmatched gusto. Every now and then she would look up and smile brightly at me. Finally, she finished typing and reached behind her desk.

"This is your new student swag!" Mrs. Fieldman exclaimed excitedly, pushing an overstuffed string backpack into my hands. "Now remember that Fridays are Hive Days, so be sure to wear all your gear to show us your school spirit!"

Apparently, Mrs. Fieldman and I had a very different idea of what was "school spirit."

"Um, Hive Days?" I asked, struggling to hold the overflowing bag.

"Ah!" Mrs. Fieldman grinned at me, as if she had been waiting her whole life for someone to ask her that question. "I am happy to announce that you are the newest member of The Swarm. We are the Chamberlain High Bumble Bees!"

Chamberlain High Bumble Bees? This had to be a joke. Why not hornets or wasps or even killer bees? I wondered how far down the list Chamberlain was when they were handing out mascots to schools. One look at the gear in the backpack confirmed it—everything was striped with black and yellow. I couldn't even imagine how ridiculous everyone looked bumbling around on Fridays.

I tried to hide my confusion. "Um, thanks. Looks like I'll have to 'bee' on my best behavior around here," I added pathetically.

The woman laughed so hard I thought she was going to rupture her spleen.

"That's the spirit!" she screeched in appreciation, handing me a schedule. "Let's see. You have 2nd lunch. There's a table for new students to mingle with some of the friendliest kids we have at school. Just follow the honeycombs to table 18. Your first class is… Intro to Psychology. Ah, fascinating! Nothing like a little dive into the human psyche." She wiggled her eyebrows at me. "That's a very popular class, you know. It may be a tiny bit crowded. Do you think you can find your way there?"

"Yes," I lied, ready to get out of the office as soon as possible. This lady's enthusiasm was starting to make me nauseous.

"Great! Good luck today, Toki. Come and stop by if you need anything," she said as she steered me toward the door and deposited me into an empty hallway.

Phew. I felt physically exhausted. I had almost forgotten how many words people said. The need to talk to the spirits was overwhelming. I resisted the urge to touch the walls, the drinking fountains, or even my swag bag. Try to be normal, I told myself. Don't be the weirdo talking to the fire extinguishers…yet. Just make it to lunch. I wondered vaguely how that was going to work. A 'special' table for new kids? I thought there weren't any new kids except for me.

I glanced at my schedule. *Intro to Psychology – Room E 216 B.*

Room E 216 B? What did that even mean? I had absolutely no idea where I was going.

There were three hallways leading in different directions. After a moment of debate, I picked the one on the left and began scanning the room numbers for any clues that I was headed the right direction.

Room A 121 C.

Room B 151 A.

The hallways were silent. It seemed like everyone was behind a closed door. It was a little unsettling, to be honest. There weren't even the habitual hall wanderers that were always going to the bathroom during every class. The building itself seemed gloomy and tired. I wanted so desperately to ask it what was wrong, but I couldn't. I had the uncomfortable feeling that I was being watched, and my stomach was abounding with indigestion.

Walking further into the darkened hallway, I noticed a bright yellow banner that seemed to be halfheartedly taped up to a glass display case. Curiously, I walked over to it.

> *RIP #11. Heaven has a new angel. We will never forget you.*

There were several pictures of the same kid covering the banner. Handsome, athletic looking type. He had a dark chiseled face. He seemed to play a multitude of sports, so he must have been talented. In one picture, he was on a field holding a football helmet in his hand. His eyes were locked on the camera with an air of confidence and gravity. I sighed—some people were just born photogenic.

There was something written on the side of his helmet. I squinted. The picture was grainy—printed from a school printer, no doubt. It was difficult to make out the letters. I felt like I was taking an eye exam.

"P… R… X… T… D… M?" I spelled aloud. "PRXTDM? What the heck does that mean?"

"It means you're terrible at spelling," a voice behind me answered.

I shrieked and spun around, swinging the swag bag blindly. It smacked into the face of a student standing behind me. He immediately collapsed down on the ground, rubbing at his nose.

"Gah! What the heck?"

I covered my mouth in horror. Great first impression, Toki. I wondered if my dad would consider attacking people as an improvement over conversing with plungers.

"I'm so sorry! Are you okay… wait a minute." My eyes narrowed suspiciously. I pointed at him accusatorily. "Were you following me?"

The boy stood up straight, grinning good-naturedly at me as he brushed off his pants. He had tousled light brown hair circling like a crown around his head, falling just past his ears. Around his neck I noticed a silver chain with a guitar pick strung in the middle. His blue eyes twinkled at me, almost as if the fact that I had just smacked him was the best part of his day.

He stuck his hand out. "Nice to meet you! Clark. Clark Kent."

I crossed my arms. "That's not your name."

He put his hand back, looking impressed. "Man, there's no getting past you, is there? You're smart. Fine fine, yeah yeah, you're right. I'm Clark Warren, your personal escort to your first class."

"You're my escort?" I asked, eyebrow raised.

He nodded enthusiastically.

"Well, no offense…"

"None taken!" he chirped.

"…but you're doing a pretty poor job of helping me get to class."

Clark shrugged. "I thought I'd let you get your bearings. Don't want you to be too dependent on me, you know? I'm not a pushy guy. Plus, you're kinda my pass to class. If you take your time getting to class, I might get to miss a quiz or something, right?"

"Let me get this straight. You followed me."

"Yup."

"Allowed me to wander around aimlessly for ten minutes."

"Mmm-hmm."

"Just so you might get out of a quiz that, if you think about it, you'd have to make up eventually."

"I know." Clark rocked on his heels, obviously proud of himself. "Great plan, right?"

I sighed. Just my luck—the first ten minutes in a new school, and I got to be personally escorted around by a weirdo with the foresight of a squirrel.

I took a good look at him. He was dressed in a nice button-up shirt, but on closer inspection, the buttons were mismatched and all in the wrong holes. I was pretty sure he was wearing two different socks, too. His backpack was slung across one shoulder, partially open, so that at any moment, all of his books could come cascading out.

What a mess. Sure, he was cute, with a lopsided smile and that carefree chestnut hair hanging just over his blue eyes. I had never met anyone that looked like him before. He looked thrown together, as if he didn't bother to consult a mirror before leaving the house. Part of me wanted to straighten his buttons and smooth his hair, but I decided that might be a little too forward the first time we met.

I cleared my throat. "Look, I just want to get to class. Which way is Room E 216 B? I'd rather not be labeled a delinquent my very first day."

"Right, right. Wait until day three for the delinquent stuff. That way you can fly under the radar for the whole year, am I right?" He raised up a hand to high-five me.

I stared back.

Clark rubbed at his head. "Ah, well. I'll take you there as soon as you tell me your name."

"Toki," I replied guardedly.

"Toe-key? That's a new one. What kind of name is that?"

"It's Japanese. My grandmother was, um, I mean is, from Japan."

"Sweet!" Clark said, rubbing his hands together. "Then what's your last name? Something cool and Japanese-y, too?"

"Um, no. My dad is straight up white. It's Tooley," I said, bracing myself for impact. "Toki Tooley."

I waited for it. The eventual joke. The giggle at my alliterative name. The snicker, no-it-can't-be-real-that-name-is-out-of-a-Dr. Seuss-book sort of comment. That was always the reaction back in my old school. Every single year, without fail. You would think that sixteen years of that type of reaction would toughen the skin, but it always got to me somehow. Ken had a normal name. I couldn't understand why my parents had to both lose their minds when I was born; one of them should have been responsible enough to realize they were making a grave mistake.

'Toki Tooley' was a ridiculous name. The spirits never thought so, but just about everybody else did.

"Ah. Well, nice to meet you, Toki Tooley!" Clark said, turning on his heels and motioning me to follow. "Let's go!"

It took a moment to register. Clark, who seemed to have no impulse control whatsoever, was completely at peace with my name.

How refreshing.

"We're going upstairs," he informed me. "Intro to Psych. Hope you're ready to read a textbook silently. Mr. Rossi's been a little... different... lately. Um, remember, if anybody happens to ask you, I was nothing but an informative, cheerful, and efficient escort for you. We'll just, ah, skip the spying part, okay?"

I glanced a little guiltily at the red spot on Clark's nose. "Sure. Can we ignore the whole assault part, too?"

"Assault? Ha! That was like a light kiss," he said, rubbing his nose a little tenderly. "With a ball peen hammer. Hopefully you don't actually kiss like that. Do you?"

I pointedly ignored him as we walked toward the elusive Room E 216 B. Before we went inside, Clark opened his mouth like he was going to say something. He then hesitated and seemed to be thinking. That must have been a novel thing for him to do. After a moment, he imperceptibly shook his head and opened the door for me.

The next moment was one of those events in life that you try to repress, shoving it deep down in your subconscious so that it can cause all sorts of problems later on. It was one of those experiences that made me seriously consider becoming a hermit in the woods and having tea parties with aspen trees the rest of my life. Walking into the silent classroom, I immediately felt thirty-five sets of eyes trained on my presence. The room was eerie; none of my classrooms had ever been this quiet before. All of the kids had gloomy faces. Some had red-rimmed puffy eyes. Others were just staring morosely at me.

The teacher, a young athletic guy with dark brown hair who was chewing on gum, stood up with effort. He crossed from his desk with heavy footsteps and smiled at me through bloodshot eyes. His shoulders slumped like he was defeated, and shaking his hand felt like waving around a wet noodle. A strange smell emanated from him, like too much aftershave.

"Ah. You're new. Toki Tooley, right?"

I nodded, unable to find any words. This place was freaking me out. From the whole classroom, there wasn't even so much as a snort at my ridiculous name. It didn't feel as relieving as it did before. Don't get me wrong - I was used to the quiet. For the most part, spirits only spoke when spoken to. That rule never seemed to apply to humans who were always talking about some inconsequential thing or another. This school, however, had a shadowy cloud settled on top of it. This silence was pervading and oppressive instead of calm and reflective.

"Great. Nice to meet you. I'm Coach Rossi. Welcome to Chamberlain High." His glazed eyes searched the classroom wearily. "It's a packed class, as you can see. Let's find you a seat."

I thought it was odd that he was consulting the seating chart so closely. There was a seat right open in the middle of the classroom next to Clark. Directly behind it sat a girl with gorgeous flowing red hair that cascaded down her back. She chewed on her fingernails aggressively, her eyes brimming with tears that were spilling on the desktop.

Finally seeming to accept defeat, Mr. Rossi lowered his clipboard. He couldn't seem to bring himself to look at the empty desk. "You can have the seat right there."

"No!" The pretty redhead dropped her fingers from her mouth. She stood up furiously as her books crashed to the ground. "You can't do that. That's HIS seat!"

Mr. Rossi looked pained, rubbing a hand over his eyes. "Sydney…"

"You just want us to forget that Liam ever existed. Now you're going to give away his seat to some stupid new kid?" She was now openly sobbing as a hand went to her mouth. "I'll never forget him. All I hear anymore is we have to move on, we have to accept he's gone. I loved him more than anything! I won't just push him away like you want me to!"

She sprinted from the room crying hysterically. Three other girls went running after her. Mr. Rossi, looking defeated and relieved all at the same time, sighed heavily.

"Okay, everyone, let's get back to work. We're reading page 77 in the textbook." He looked at me as if he had just remembered I was still standing in the front of class awkwardly. Giving me the weakest smile in the history of ever, he said, "Go ahead and have a seat, Toki. It's just a chair, right?"

Yeah, easy for him to say. Everyone watched silently as I shuffled clumsily to the middle of the room and sat down with trepidation. Even the desk groaned as if it couldn't believe I was sitting there. We'd have to have a conversation about that later, I told myself. It didn't seem I was making a good impression with anyone today. Well except for Clark, who caught my eye and gave me an encouraging smile.

Everyone had a textbook. I glanced around and found one under the desk. I opened the cover. There was a series of interesting but not entirely accurate doodles of the human anatomy on the first page. I glanced at the names that were written inside the front cover—everyone the book had ever been assigned to.

That's when I saw it. The breath escaped my lungs in an instant. At the bottom of the list written in nice, legible printed letters:

Liam Paxton.

I recognized the name like it had been burned into my memory. Paxton from Grandmother's journal. I had found him.

A STEADY STREAM of students hurried toward the cafeteria for lunch, heads down and talking in quiet packs. It was all too unfamiliar to me—no obnoxious mobs of burly and loud teenagers shouting insults, cursing, and spitting. The air was tense and morose like everyone was sleep walking through a boring dream. Everything from the lockers to the motivational posters felt dark and heavy. I knew what I had promised my dad, but I also knew what I had to do. I just had to make sure I wasn't seen.

I dawdled behind the crowds and revisited the yellow banner in an empty hallway. Liam Paxton. I knew his full name now. No wonder Clark had doubted if I was literate. Now that I knew who Liam was, I was curious to know more about him. Why was my Grandmother writing about him in her journal right before she handed it to me?

Looking around to make sure I was truly alone, I closed my eyes and placed a hand on one of Liam's picture.

Gone, gone.

I gasped, pulling my hand away. The spirit sounded exactly the same as that night I had heard the ground cry out. Very rarely do spirits say the same thing. They are like us, and their personalities are complex and unique. To have two spirits say the exact same thing in the same distressed tone made me nervous. No wonder the school felt so oppressive. Everything was connected to Liam Paxton.

He had obviously died somehow. Judging from the reaction of Sydney in 1st hour, it had been recently. No wonder everyone had lost their minds when I took his seat. It was like I was sitting on a ghost. Taking Liam's seat must have driven home the fact for everyone that he was gone forever.

I stared at the picture closer. He was good-looking. Even looking at the picture made me blush a bit. He seemed athletic, popular. Having only kept to myself and the spirits, I wondered what it would be like to be in his shoes. Everyone liking you, going out on dates, going to other people's houses to hang out—that was all foreign to me. My brother Ken knew all about that; he made it seem like he would rather spend time with anyone else except his weirdo family.

"How did you end up in Grandmother Emi's journal?" I asked the picture quietly. I pulled it out from my jacket pocket where I had kept it since my strange visit.

2. 03

D: L. Paxton (17) STU - CHS

Okay, so maybe I could decode this now. The D stood for deceased or dead. The date was the exact same night I had heard the spirits crying out. He must have died that night.

I frowned. Did Grandmother Emi have a habit of trying to record the death of people around this town? This place wasn't exactly a thriving metropolis if she was some sort of true crime reporter. I remembered a billboard outside of town that supported the local sheriff for reelection mentioned that this was one of the safest towns in the country. If so, why were there so many entries in the journal?

One thing was for certain. Liam Paxton was dead. He was a student here at Chamberlain High School, and judging from the journal, he was seventeen years old when he died. I thought of Ken. He was only a year or so older than Liam. They were so similar. The thought of Ken dying at such a young age took the breath out of my lungs. It wouldn't be fair, I thought to myself. You're supposed to die when you're old, not before you've been able to really live your own life.

I bit my lip and looked at his picture one last time.

"What happened to you?" I asked.

Chapter Four: Best Buzzer

THE GREAT EQUALIZER in all high schools across America is the lunchroom. It doesn't matter what school you came from or what school you're going to. The cafeteria is a never-ending stream of technology, gossip, and (most frightening to me) human interaction. Despite all that, being in a lunchroom when you're a brand new student is as an anxiety-inducing experience as you can get. I looked down at the floor and noticed neon-yellow honeycomb stickers across the linoleum. Mrs. Fieldman had mentioned something about going to table 18 for some of the friendliest kids in school. That gave me some hope. Being socially awkward, I was never one to do well with initiating conversation. Friendly, outgoing, socially-adjusted kids, however, should have that down to a science. The prospect of meeting some normal kids, especially considering how my day had gone so far, was intriguing.

I stopped dead in my tracks when I saw Clark waving wildly at me from across the cafeteria. The honeycomb stickers were a trap. They were leading directly to his table.

"You've got to be kidding me," I grumbled.

I approached the table of the "friendliest" kids—there were only three of them, and they didn't seem to be talking much to each other. A girl stood up and stuck out her hand forcefully. If she was trying to be friendly and welcoming, she must have taken lessons from a guard dog. She had beautiful, flawless dark brown skin like a model, but everything on her face read that greeting me was against all of her personal beliefs. She towered over me, her springy ringlet hair bouncing up and down when she moved. She looked as graceful and slender as a ballet dancer, but there was also a dangerous intensity about her. She seemed like a dormant volcano ready to explode at any moment. I took note to watch myself.

"Hi," she said, flatly and clearly rehearsed. "I'm Nichelle Tyler. Nice to meet you. Welcome to Chamberlain High School. What's your name? Where are you from?"

She sounded like she was reading a teleprompter from the back of the room. There was clearly no real interest in her expression. I carefully shook her outstretched hand, wincing as my own hand was crushed under a grip of steel. She looked like she wanted to fight someone. Maybe even me.

"I'm Toki. I just moved here from Oregon," I squeaked back at her.

"Back off, Nichelle!" Clark interrupted. "I already escorted her to class this morning. You've basically already lost."

Nichelle shot a look back at Clark that could've melted a glacier. "Whatever. She has the final say, not you." She looked at me with a glimmer of threat smoldering in her dark brown eyes. "Who knows? She might be smart enough to pick me."

As I sat down, I glanced at the other kid at the table. He was an Asian kid with jet black hair styled with brassy yellow spikes that reminded me of old manga-books my mom used to read. Dressed in a dark hoodie that seemed to swallow him up, he seemed oddly apart even from the other two. He was staring at the floor and clearly uninterested in what was happening.

"What exactly am I picking?" I asked tentatively.

"We're the Buzzers," Clark informed me. "We are the... uh... what's the word? Oh! We are the representatives for the new kids in school. Which you're the only one we've had in forever, basically. Anyway, after a week at school, you have to pick who was the most friendly, outgoing, helpful, and handsome..."

Nichelle snorted.

"...of the Buzzers group. Then that person gets a special, well... prize, I guess."

"What's the prize?" I asked.

Clark and Nichelle glanced at each other for a moment uncertainly.

"Well," Clark began delicately, choosing his words with the utmost care, "the Buzzer that has been chosen by you will have shown immense growth and maturity, earning the title of Best Buzzer. And so..."

"The prize is getting out of lunch detention," Nichelle finished.

"Wait, what?" I was baffled. "You're telling me this is the lunch detention table? Mrs. Fieldman said this table is for new students."

Clark shrugged. "New kid table, bad kid table—here at Chamberlain, it's all the same. Think about this though, Toki. If you pick me, then you and I can go to any table we want in the lunch room! I can introduce you to anyone. They all know me here. You think Grouchy-Pants Nichelle can do that? No way. Everyone's afraid of her."

"For good reason," Nichelle responded with a hint of pride in her voice.

I had to process this out loud. "Let me get this straight. To encourage you guys to be on your best behavior, you're stuck in lunch detention until a new kid picks you as... what, a friend? Doesn't it seem a little strange to basically throw new kids in with the... ah..." I struggled to find a positive euphemism for my thoughts but was finding nothing.

"The delinquents?" Clark suggested.

"I'm not a delinquent!" Nichelle insisted, sitting down and chewing on a sandwich aggressively. "I was reminding a kid to keep my name out of his mouth. Then I punched him when he couldn't learn. Is that a crime?"

"Depends on how hard you punched," I murmured.

Clark slid in the seat next to me. "Oh, she punches hard, trust me. Now me, I'm truly innocent. I'm in lunch detention forever because of a simple misunderstanding."

"He played his band's first recorded track over the morning announcements instead of reciting the Pledge of Allegiance," Nichelle informed me.

"I was trying to get us some free airtime. Is that a crime?"

"Depends on how bad the music was," I responded.

Nichelle rolled her eyes. "Oh, it was bad. Trust me."

I glanced at the other student, eyes still locked on the floor. "What's his story?"

"That's Peter," Clark informed me. "He's been a Buzzer since the beginning of time. He probably will be forever because he doesn't talk to anyone. Getting him to talk to a new kid would be like trying to squeeze a conversation out of a rock."

That's not as hard as you think, I thought to myself.

Clark was rattling on. "I think he's in here for hacking the school's network or something. He's like an evil genius in training, but that's only if he ever makes it out of detention. Can't be plotting against the world when you're banned from using your phone at lunch, right Peter?"

Without looking up, Peter flipped Clark off for a full five seconds before returning to his own impassive state.

Clark grinned. "I think he likes me."

These people are insane, I thought to myself. As Clark and Nichelle were distracted arguing about who was getting out of detention first, I put my hand on the table and tried to listen. Maybe it could give me some insight into what these Buzzers were all about. I listened, but the table remained silent. That was frustrating. Usually I could coax a spirit into talking—cleaning it with antibacterial wipes would probably have done the trick, but I had left my bag of offerings at home.

A commotion in the corner of the lunchroom stopped everyone's conversation. A group of girls was gathered around teary-eyed Sydney as she walked in the cafeteria. They all sat down at a table and took turns consoling her as she sobbed into a tissue.

Clark shook his head sympathetically. "Sydney. It's her first day back at school since her boyfriend died."

"Liam," I said absentmindedly.

Nichelle and Clark stared at me, surprised.

"How did you know that?" she demanded.

I avoided her question. Somehow bringing up the topic of my crime-obsessed grandmother and my conversations with the spirits seemed like a bad idea on my first day.

"What happened to him?" I asked.

"About a week ago, they found him on the side of the road," Clark said, noticeably uncomfortable. "It was right after a big wrestling meet, so it was pretty late. There was this crazy snowstorm that came in and dumped a ton of snow and ice on the roads. Talk about bad luck. His motorcycle broke down, and he was trying to fix it. They think someone hit him and drove off without realizing what they had done."

The sound of raised voices came from across the cafeteria. A stocky boy wearing a hideously colored yellow and black striped athletic jacket had walked up to Sydney. He tried to say something to her. She stood up angrily and was shouting back at him, pointing her finger accusingly. He started to yell back, though I couldn't understand what they were saying over the terrible acoustics in the lunchroom. It all sounded like an angry jumble. Eventually, a girl with a dark pixie hair cut pulled the boy away from the crowd and led him outside. Sydney shouted something at him as he left then stormed out of the cafeteria with her crowd of friends trailing after her.

"Who was that guy?"

"That," Nichelle said with obvious disdain in her voice, "is the reason I'm in the stupid Buzzers club to begin with. Mike Treverly. Couldn't stop talking about me whenever I walked past him. I gave him a reminder to stop. Of course, everybody—even the dean!—sees his side of the story. They act like I randomly assaulted him or something. Now here I am, forced to be nice to all the stupid new kids."

"Thanks," I frowned. "So what's up with Sydney and Mike? Why are they fighting?"

"Can't imagine why they would have a problem with each other. Mike was Liam's best friend. They were all part of this little circle of chums before all this. Sydney's been pretty sensitive lately, so who knows?" Clark observed as he tilted his head, draining the last crumbs in a bag of chips into his mouth.

There was something curious about those two. I had heard that deaths usually drew people closer together, but this entire place - the school, the town itself, even the spirits - seemed fractured and devastated by Liam's death. What was going on here? Is this why Grandmother Emi was investigating?

It was obvious that she spoke to the spirits like I did. Perhaps she had felt the darkness the night that Liam died. I had never known spirits to react so strongly to the death of a human, but then again, I hadn't ever known anyone who died. Was it possible that finding out why he died would bring some peace to the spirits around Devil's Ford?

Grandmother Emi couldn't investigate, not in her current state, anyway. The reason she had given me the journal was suddenly starting to make more sense. She wanted me to take up the cause and find out who killed Liam.

I didn't know whether to feel honored or horrified.

Either way, it was obvious that I would never get the answers. I wasn't exactly a social butterfly, and being a new kid didn't help my cause. The only people who would talk to me were only doing it because they desperately needed me to get out of detention. How could I get any information about Liam and his death?

I stared down at the lunch table, still bitter because it wouldn't talk to me. If only I had brought my bag of offerings like I always did…

Offerings.

I suddenly had an idea. Dangerous, but it could work, especially if spirit-bartering logic worked with humans.

"Want to make a deal?" I asked.

Clark and Nichelle looked up at me, interested. Peter's eyes were still glued to the ground.

"I want to know more about what happened to Liam."

Nichelle looked at me incredulously, her dark eyes narrowing. "What? Are you some sort of sicko? The kid's dead. What more do you need to know?"

Time for the offering—just like with some stubborn spirits, I had to up the ante.

"And," I added, ignoring her question, "whoever can help me the most will be my pick for Best Buzzer."

They both stared at me. Clark whistled, impressed.

"Oh man, Toki, you really know how to play the game! Count me in." He threw a cocky grin in Nichelle's direction. "Look who's going to be paroled early. Hope you enjoy waiting another ten years for a new kid to come!"

Nichelle crossed her arms, annoyed. "Okay. You want to be nosy, fine. If that's what it takes, I can help you find out something. Clark's as useful as a used Q-tip. Best Buzzer is as good as mine."

As the lunch bell rang, I watched the students slowly file out of the cafeteria heading back to their classes. I felt a little proud of myself. Maybe interacting with humans and spirits wasn't as different as I had imagined.

Little did I know, I was getting in way over my head in something I didn't completely understand.

"How was school?" Dad asked me as we sat around the dinner table. We were surrounded by moving boxes like we were the occupants of a cardboard castle under siege.

I knew what he was really trying to ask. *Did you act normal today, or did you have a conversation with a stapler?*

I stared at the greasy piece of pizza on the paper plate in front of me. "Fine."

"Make any new friends?" Mom asked optimistically.

Good question. "Well, I sat at the new kids' table, which turned out to also be the lunch detention table. The kids in detention are basically forced to be my friend in order to get sprung."

"That's nice," Dad replied absently as he dug through a box trying to find the salt and pepper shakers. "I swear this is the last time I get Ken to pack. Today I found the spoons in a box with the motor oil."

Mom threw him a look. "That's very interesting about your day, Toki, but you know you should make good choices about your friends out here. You don't have to be friends with those kids in detention. It's a program the school has to help… well, you know…"

"Loser new kids with no friends?" I suggested.

Mom pursed her lips which usually meant I was right. "All I'm trying to say is you have a chance to start over. You can be whatever and whoever you want to be. You're perfectly capable of making your own friends. You're a smart, talented, and thoughtful young woman. You don't need to take the easy way out."

"Although," my dad added, "it'd be nice to have conversations with real people once in awhile instead of inanimate objects, wouldn't it?"

I sighed as I stood up from the table. "Yeah, I get it, Dad."

"Remember that you promised to work on Wednesday at the

day care, pumpkin! We have a lot of clients signed up for the grand opening," Dad called to me as I exited to my room.

I looked at Mom imploringly. "You just said I'm a talented young woman. You don't count scooping dog poop all afternoon as a waste of my talents?"

She shook her head with a smirk. "Sorry sweetie. That just comes with the territory when your dad owns a doggy day care."

I sighed. What rotten luck. "How was Grandmother Emi today?" I asked, trying to mask my curiosity with a casual indifference.

Mom pulled her long black hair back from her face. Lines of worry creased at the corners of her eyes as she rested her head in her hands, elbows on the table. "Nothing new," she said in a quiet voice. "I wonder if she'll ever wake up at this rate."

There she went again into her deep silence that could fill the Grand Canyon whenever she mentioned her mother. Part of me wanted to ask her what was wrong, and the other part of me wanted to confess everything that had happened on Sunday. In the end I just ended up going to my room. It was the only space in the entire house that wasn't a complete disaster as I had already unpacked all of my things. I went over to my bed and pulled out the journal from my pocket.

Rule one: the clock is both your enemy and your...

"Yeah, yeah, I know," I said dismissively, opening to Liam's page.

---

2. 03
D: L. Paxton (17) STU - CHS
C.S. 1800 Delta Rd., f. 8:33 P.M.
H & R ???
TT nr bdy
Blnt f. Trma
Phone???

Some things were beginning to make sense now. It was safe to assume that C.S stood for "crime scene." Liam had been found at Delta Road at around half past eight the night of the 3rd. H & R also made sense. Grandmother Emi was questioning whether Liam's death was actually a hit and run. There was blunt force trauma to Liam, and it seemed like there was some issue with Liam's phone. Maybe it was missing?

I couldn't help but think about Liam's picture as I read over his death. Everything about this was grim and uncertain. I could understand why Grandmother had questioned if this was a hit and run. For the spirits of an entire town to be so affected, something truly tragic must have happened.

The longer I held the journal, I noticed something peculiar. A thin line of white light, barely perceptible, was seeping from the journal and doing figure 8's around my wrists. I stared at it. It was like it was tying itself to me. I threw the journal on the floor, and the light disappeared.

I took a shaky breath. My life and this case were becoming intertwined, and I didn't think it was by accident. If the clock was my friend and my enemy as the journal kept insisting, I couldn't just sit around and hope the answers would conveniently fall into my lap.

I knew what I had promised my dad, but I needed some extra help. Tomorrow, for sure, I was bringing my bag of offerings with me to school. I had a feeling I would need as much help as I could get from spirits and humans alike.

Chapter Five: Breaking and Entering

Tuesday, February 9th. 4:12 p.m.

AFTER 4. The track field. Don't tell that idiot Clark.

That's all Nichelle's note said that she slipped me during lunch, which I thought was pretty fitting based on the short time that I had known her. The wind was whipping round wildly outside and making a cold day even more unbearable. I shivered in my heavy winter jacket. Leave it to Nichelle to pick the most uncomfortable meeting spot ever.

She finally came jogging up, a big backpack slung across her shoulder bouncing heavily against her. Her beautiful ringlets of hair were tied back showing the flawlessness of her dark skin. I felt a pang of jealousy and thought self-consciously about my own skin. It was raw, red, chapped, and blotchy. I watched as in a graceful bound, she motioned me over to a side door of the school. It had been propped open nearly invisibly with a small rock. We slipped inside the door, standing just inside a darkened passageway.

"What's this all about?" I asked, wiping at my defrosting nose.

Nichelle glanced around the empty hallways. "These are the athletic locker rooms. Only for students who do after school sports. This is the last place Liam was before he died. There was a big wrestling meet that night. Get this—Mike, Sydney, and Liam were all there."

I wrinkled my nose. "Okay… but why are we here?"

Nichelle glared at my lack of appreciation for her plan. "If you just want gossip, go stand at the bathroom mirrors for an hour. You'll hear the truth, and you'll hear lies. You'll also have no idea what to believe and what not to believe. If there's anything juicy, it may be in here."

That was a good point. Plus Nichelle looked increasingly annoyed at me, so I nodded my head compliantly.

With one more look around, she waved me to the entrance of the Boys' Athletic Locker Room. Pulling a key from her pocket, she quietly unlocked it. Noticing my raised eyebrow, she smiled smugly.

"Got this from Coach Rossi's keys. He leaves them lying around everywhere. It's a copy."

I had to admit that I was impressed with her planning. Who would have thought someone would be so motivated to get out of detention? It made sense, though. Being a happy, friendly, welcoming Buzzer must have been torture for the surly-looking Nichelle.

The locker room was dark and smelled faintly of bleach and sweaty boy. It was pitch black, illuminated only by the light on our cell phones. Nichelle locked the door behind me.

"The only problem is we need to find Liam's locker," she admitted, blowing a ringlet out of her face. "It might take a while, so we gotta work fast."

"How are we going to open it when we find it?" I asked.

Reaching into her backpack, she brandished the biggest pair of bolt cutters I'd ever seen.

"Whoa. Where'd you get those?"

She shrugged nonchalantly. "One of my aunts owns a storage facility. This is how they get the crap out of people's units when they don't pay up."

Okay. I could see Nichelle's plan clearly. She was going to snip off every lock, one by one, until she found Liam's locker. Not only would it be time consuming, but it would be pretty obvious that someone had been in there tampering with the lockers. One look at the security camera footage, and we'd be toast. I shook my head.

"Wait a minute," I said.

I placed my hand on a locker, listening.

"What are you doing?" Nichelle asked impatiently.

I waved her away. The locker took a moment, but finally responded.

No.

"Thank you," I murmured, moving to the next locker.

No.

It's wrong.

No.

No.

Gone, gone.

I stopped. Nichelle was watching me with a frown, tapping her foot.

"This one," I said, pointing, "is Liam's locker."

"How do you know?" she demanded.

I didn't answer, partially because I knew I couldn't, but I was also thinking about all the lockers' answers. *It's wrong?* Why not just *no?*

After a hesitation, I pointed to the different locker. "I'm pretty sure that one is Mike's."

Nichelle, almost beside herself to prove me wrong, snipped the lock in half like it was made out of butter. She pulled off the combination lock and threw it in her backpack. When she opened the door, she pulled out an athletic jacket inside and looked at the name stitched on the back.

"Paxton. It is his," she murmured, amazed. "How did you possibly..."

"No time, remember?" I said, cutting her off. "Check to see if that one is Mike's. I'll look through this one."

As Nichelle focused her attention on the other locker, I took my phone and shone the light around the inside. I reached into the pockets of his jacket. I tried to ignore the feeling that I was doing something terribly wrong in rifling through a dead kid's things.

Gone, gone, the jacket said mournfully.

I know, I thought sympathetically. Also gone was Liam's cell phone. Not here, not on him when he died—where could it be?

There was a mess at the bottom of the locker: torn-up bits of paper, an upturned bag of sunflower seeds, two wilted, wrinkly flower petals, and an empty prescription bottle. I picked up everything and shoved it in my offerings bag. There was no time to decide what was important and what wasn't. I would have to sort through it all later.

I crept over to Nichelle, who was staring at the other locker as she threw the second snipped-off combination lock into her bag.

"I just don't believe it. You found both lockers on a lucky guess."

"Yup, lucky guess," I muttered, picking up a piece of paper that had fluttered out.

Nichelle looked over the rest of the locker with disappointment. "Nothing's here. I was hoping that creep Treverly might have some dirt on him."

I waved the paper triumphantly. "Your wish has been granted. Listen to this."

In plain but neat handwriting, the note read:

Mike,

I thought I'd leave this here since you've decided not to return my calls or texts anymore. I know that you used me like a puppet. I feel stupid, but most of all I feel responsible. Please do something before it's too late.

"Scandalous! Keep that note. I'll bet Sydney wrote it, and that's why they're fighting," Nichelle said, digging into her backpack as she handed me a brand new, open combination lock. "Here. Put that back on Liam's locker so we can cover our tracks. No one will ever know we were in here."

Impressed with her continued foresight, I snapped the new lock back on. "How many of these did you bring?"

"Enough. It cost me a fortune, but that was before I knew you'd be all psychic and guess the right lockers. I can still return the ones we didn't use at the store though, so it's all cool."

"Geez, remind me to never get on your bad side. What happens when Mike tries to get back into his locker? It's going to be a different combination."

I saw Nichelle's face light up with the brightest smile I'd ever seen from her. "I know. Shame I won't be here to witness it. Think of the big, stupid, hulking brute trying over and over to open a lock that's never going to budge! This is almost worth all the money I spent buying these locks. Now, let's get out of here before someone…"

The sound of heavy footsteps approaching from the outside door made us freeze. The unmistakable jangling of keys made my stomach drop.

"Hide!" Nichelle hissed at me. Attempting to run as quietly as I could in clunky winter boots, I followed her as we bolted into the nearest toilet stalls and shut the doors. I climbed up on the toilet seat which looked like it hadn't been properly cleaned in a month. I held my breath because 1.) I didn't trust myself to breathe quietly at this moment and 2.) The overpowering stench of a boys' toilet was making me feel faint. I placed my hands tightly against the sides of the stall so I wouldn't fall down.

Clean? The stall wall asked hopefully through its markings of crude sharpie sketches and phone numbers.

Not today, I thought apologetically. I didn't blame it at all for asking.

The overhead lights flicked on, and a blinding cascade of fluorescent light scorched my eyes. Whoever had entered the room was talking on the phone. Hopefully he hadn't heard Nichelle and me beforehand. The tired voice echoed off of the concrete walls of the locker room.

"No, I just… no, listen. We're done. I did what you asked."

A pause.

"Well, how do you think I'm doing? I'm devastated, I'm lost. I'm worried. We all are in way over our heads. It's high time to end it. If anybody finds out about the… well, you got what you wanted, didn't you?"

Whoever it was sounded familiar. I closed my eyes. Coach Rossi? Yes, it was definitely him! There was something different about his voice. It was louder, almost lacking in refined control. His words were slightly slurring together.

He walked past the row of toilet stalls, pacing back and forth.

"I know. I know! You won't hear anything more from me, but I want to tell you I'm out. …I'm worried that I might have done something very wrong." A loud thud reverberated throughout the room as he headed back toward the staff offices.

There was a jangling of keys. A heavy door opened and shut. Coach Rossi's voice became muffled again.

I heard Nichelle knock on the side of the stall quietly. "Toki! Let's go."

I reached into my bag of offerings and pulled out a cloth and disinfectant spray kept just for situations like this. I quickly sprayed the wall and gave it a quick wipe, hoping that was enough pampering to help the poor stall through its crisis moment. As I stepped out, Nichelle stared at me, unbelieving.

"What are you doing… cleaning?! Hurry up before he comes back out again."

We seemed to have a clear way out. I could still hear the rise and fall of Rossi's voice in his office behind a door. I desperately wanted to hear the rest of the phone call, but spending the night in the faintly pee-and-boy-smelling locker room did not appeal to me in the slightest.

As I followed Nichelle, I stopped. Something in the air was humming. It was a sound I'd recognized anywhere. Something desperately wanted to talk to me.

"What are you doing? Let's go?"

I searched around. What was it? The spirit was humming louder, almost begging to be noticed. I had to find it. A spirit who wanted to talk that badly surely had something important to say.

That's when I found it. The trash can by the bathroom stalls. It was practically rattling.

I put my hand on it. Silence. The spirit was waiting for something with anticipation.

"Okay, I get it," I whispered. I took the rag and spray bottle and cleaned the top and the sides of the trash can thoroughly.

"Have you gone insane?" Nichelle exclaimed as quietly as she could.

After a quick but effective wipe down, I put my hand back on the trash can's lid.

Look inside, it whispered graciously.

I stuck my hand into the trash can blindly as Nichelle made gagging noises behind me. A strange smell emanated. My hand almost instantly wrapped around something cool and heavy. When I pulled it out, I understood what the trash can was trying to say and what that peculiar smell was.

I was holding a giant bottle of vodka. It was completely empty.

Moderation, the bottle groaned at me.

Nichelle blinked. "Whoa."

I put the bottle back in the trash can, and we slipped out the door carefully stealing into the waning light of the day. Moving as quietly as possible, we strode away from the school. It was even colder than it had been fifteen minutes ago. As the wind bit against my face with a new violence, Nichelle turned to me. She looked like she had questions, but she didn't quite know how to phrase them. I decided to take the initiative. Maybe she would forget the whole incident with the offerings.

"He was wasted. I could definitely smell it as he walked by. I wonder who he was talking to. He mentioned that he might have done something wrong..."

I froze in my footsteps, putting pieces together.

"Yeah, that's all well and good Toki, but what the heck is going on with you and that cleaning getup? Are you some sort of germaphobe?"

The bottle. The guilt-ridden, tense stretch of his voice. A vague picture was beginning to swirl around my head. The hit and run. Liam, left for dead out in the middle of a blizzard, his body broken by someone too scared to stop. Or was it someone too drunk to notice?

"Nichelle," I said a little breathlessly as the thoughts gathered in my head like storm clouds. The power of my words was beginning to frighten me. "Do you think Coach Rossi had something to do with Liam's death? What if he was drunk that night, hit him, and didn't even realize it before it was too late?"

Nichelle's mouth opened, but nothing came out. Her eyes widened at the thought.

Finally, she said, "Well, maybe. I mean the alcohol and the phone call. Maybe." Suddenly, her eyes hardened. "Wait a minute. Why do you care about all of this anyway? You some sort of junior detective? You didn't even know Liam. Honestly you don't even know anyone. It's none of your business."

I couldn't believe what she was saying. The very spirits of this town were crying out in anguish over Liam's death, and she was acting like it didn't concern anyone.

"Don't you want to know what happened to him?" I asked incredulously. "He was your classmate. He was just left there to die!"

"Yeah, I know. But here's something you weren't around to know. Liam Paxton was a jerk. He was spoiled rotten, he got whatever he wanted, and he definitely didn't care for anyone like you or me," Nichelle growled. Her fists were clenched.

I watched her, dumbstruck.

"That whole group, all of his friends, they don't care who they step on, who they insult, who they hurt. Life is one big popularity contest. If you're lucky, you're invisible to them. If you're not, well, they make it their mission to make your life a living hell. Toki, you would have hated him if you had known him. He probably would've hated you, too. To answer your question, no, I don't care what happened to Liam. You shouldn't. You should be thankful you never had to deal with him."

I shook my head earnestly. "You can't actually mean that! I mean, maybe he was a bad person. I don't know, but I do know that he didn't deserve to die like that. Nobody does."

"Girl, listen to me. It's not your problem. Bad stuff happens all the time, and if you try to run around and fix it all, you're going to miss your own life." She glared at me, gesturing toward my spray bottle and rag which were still in my hands. "Maybe you should spend more time making friends or trying to be normal instead of snooping around like some crime-solving janitor. The sooner you can get real friends, the sooner you and I can go our separate ways."

I huffed, shoving my cleaning offerings into my bag. "Fine. You're okay with kids getting randomly mowed over in your town. I get it. No wonder you sit at the detention table all by yourself."

Her dark eyes blazed indignantly. I flinched slightly, preparing my face to be rearranged by her fists. Surprisingly, she didn't try to destroy me. Maybe her anger management classes were working. More likely, she didn't think I was worth the effort of the extra detention she would get for maiming the new kid.

"Don't forget your end of the deal!" she barked, pointing her finger at me threateningly. "You would've never even gotten in to that locker room if it weren't for me."

I shrugged nonchalantly, walking away. "Maybe. You never know. Clark might find something more useful. It is a competition, remember?"

Nichelle laughed at the thought of that. She shouldered her backpack roughly. "Yeah right. You want to hang out with that spaz, be my guest. Clark's about as useful as a zit. He'll never find anything. You need to stop wasting everyone's time before you become a reject like all of us."

With that said, she stomped off into the opposite direction.

I took a deep breath. That wasn't a great start to my investigation or to my crusade to be 'normal'. I glanced at my bag, knowing I had a full night ahead of me to try to make sense of what I found in the locker room. It seemed like my only win for today was the fact that I still had an intact jawbone after personally facing Nichelle's wrath.

Chapter Six: Mardi Paws

Wednesday, February 10th. 8:03 a.m.

IF I WEREN'T SO BRAND NEW, so recognizable, and sitting squat in the middle of the dead kid's desk, I probably would've skipped Coach Rossi's class the next morning. I even considered trying to act like I was sick so I could stay home. Fat chance of that working. Today was the grand opening of Mardi Paws, my dad's doggy day care. Even if I had the plague and was bleeding out of every orifice of my body, my dad would expect me to be there scooping poo with a customer-friendly smile in my ridiculous green-and-purple uniform with an obnoxious graphic of a bulldog wearing beads on the front. Yeah. Mardi Paws. Great one, dad.

No, pretending to be ill was not an option. However, sitting in Coach Rossi's class that morning made me feel nauseous. I could only remember his words from yesterday. *I'm worried that I might have done something very wrong.*

Coach Rossi was even more nonverbal that class than usual. On the board, he had written directions for us to silently read a chapter in the psych book about how the human brain processes emotions. I couldn't focus on a single word. Instead, I found myself looking over the top of the book at my teacher who sat morosely in front of the class at his desk. His eyes were sunken and blood red. When I first met him I thought that he just looked tired, but now I knew better. Thanks to a needy trash can, I knew he was hung over, maybe even possibly still drunk from last night. The gum-chewing, the overwhelming aroma of aftershave—it was all an attempt to cover up the smell of alcohol. I couldn't have been the first one to notice this.

My eyes drilled a hole into his fatigued face. He didn't even look up once. Was Coach Rossi a killer? It probably wasn't intentional. Still, if Rossi even thought for a moment he could have killed Liam, even if he wasn't completely sure, shouldn't he have gone to the police? Unless he was trying to cover it up. In that case, Grandmother Emi had a right to be suspicious about Liam's death.

That was only half the problem. There were so many secrets about Liam's life that I was still trying to understand. I glanced in my bag which now held my spirit offerings, the black journal, and the contents of yesterday's break-in. Instead of sleeping like normal people might do, I had stayed up into the wee hours of the morning diligently taping back together the torn-up pieces of paper that were at the bottom of Liam's locker. Its contents were another intriguing puzzle.

February 3rd

Dear Mr. and Mrs. Paxton,

I regret to inform you after receiving an anonymous tip from our Safe-to-Say line, an unannounced locker search was conducted on all athletes' lockers. I personally found narcotics in Liam's possession that were not prescribed to him—a quantity of which I believe he is intending to distribute. As you may be aware, this is a serious violation of the athletic code of conduct as well as potentially having severe legal consequences.

As I have tried the home phone number in the school system and received no response, I find it necessary to send this notification home with Liam to be hand-delivered. Your student will not be charged at this point in time, though he will face immediate suspension from any athletic or extra-curricular activity until the investigation has concluded. At that time, charges may be filed.

I urge you to contact me at your earliest convenience to update your contact information and discuss this matter further with the principal, athletic director, coaches, and school security team.

Sincerely,
Coach Anthony Rossi

Something about this letter seemed wrong to me, but I couldn't for the life of me explain why. Any attempt to talk to it failed as well, as it only whined *Anger, unfair* when I tried to coax anything useful.

The empty pill bottle wasn't any more helpful. When I tried to talk to it, it only chanted at me *Use as directed!* This was what any medication usually said, so I figured as much. It had a torn label, so I wasn't able to make out who the prescription was originally for. There was a tiny part of the label left, and because of that, I knew what was missing from the bottle. Vicodin was a drug I had heard about in my old school. Kids would sell it to each other, especially the athletes, to dull sore and aching muscles and get a quick high.

Liam was accused of selling Vicodin. From what the letter implied, he was suspended from sports for an indefinite amount of time. Something about it all didn't quite add up.

If he was suspended from sports that day, why was he at the wrestling meet the night he died? Why was the letter all torn up and at the bottom of his athletic locker? If all this pill nonsense wasn't true, I would imagine Liam would take it home, show it to his parents, and have them fight the good fight to get him back on the wrestling team. If Liam was as promising of an athlete as I thought he was, why wouldn't Coach Rossi fight tooth and nail to wait until his parents had been notified before the suspension occurred?

I furrowed my brow, resuming my gaze on Rossi. He was blinking heavily and looking a little unsteady in his chair. Instead of Liam's death becoming more straightforward as I thought it would, there were little threads unraveling my theories. I had to follow them all to see where they were going. I made a mental note of the next steps I had to take as I chewed my pencil.

"He's married, you know," Clark informed me in a low voice, elbowing me back into the real world.

"Wha-?" I jumped and looked around. We were the only ones in the classroom. The bell must have rung without me hearing it. Coach Rossi still sat staring blankly from behind his desk.

I blushed a thousand different shades of red and gathered all of my papers, shoving them hastily into my bag. We quickly exited the classroom. Clark was close on my heels.

"Well, I just thought I'd let you know," he continued. "I mean you were staring at him pretty much the whole class."

I huffed. "I wasn't staring at him because I like him, you creep." I stopped and turned around to face him accusingly. "What exactly were you doing watching *me* the whole time, hmmm?"

Clark put up his hands defensively as his face broke down into a guilty smile. "Whoa, calm down. I was watching you because I was trying to get your attention all class, but you were too busy making lovey-gooey eyes at Rossi. Geez, I'm not a stalker, you know."

I rolled my eyes as I stomped down the hallway. "Yeah, not a stalker. Even though I seem to remember that you were literally following me around silently the first day of school…"

"Okay, when you put it that way, it does sound pretty bad."

"Anyway," I continued, not in the mood for Clark's excuses, "I'm not into our teacher. I'm investigating him. I think he might have something to do with Liam's death. Haven't you noticed he's completely wasted or hung over every time he teaches? Is it so far-fetched to think he might have accidentally killed Liam that night?"

Clark blinked his blue eyes excitedly, grabbing at my arm. "What, you're serious? You're a detective? Like Batman? Oh man, oh man, oh man…. Pleeeease! You have to let me help you. I've always wanted to be Batman!"

I thought about the next steps in my investigation. "Maybe you can help. Do you have a car?"

Clark grinned. "Do I ever! What else do you need? Grappling hook? Magnetic suit? A BATARANG?"

"Clark, calm down. I need you to take me somewhere. Can you show me where it happened?"

He tilted his head at me. "What do you mean?"

"I need to go to the place where Liam died."

WE AGREED TO MEET at the coffee shop down the street from my house at 7:00 p.m., which I figured would give me plenty of time to close down the doggy day care for the night, change out of my hideous work uniform (the bead-covered bull dog was definately not an outfit I'd wear out in public), and get cleaned up to go to the crime scene on Delta Road. It was going to be dark by that time. I wasn't exactly sure why I was going there, but something was telling me I had to see the place where Liam had spent his last moments alive.

Clark assured me that he had the coolest vehicle in town which left me slightly curious about what would be pulling into the coffee shop. Knowing Clark for the short amount of time I had, it was probably a Segway or something equally as obnoxious.

As I wandered around cleaning up the dog play area of Mardi Paws,

I felt pretty proud of myself. I had planned everything out rather nicely. However, it all fell apart as, mid-scoop into a giant piece of fresh dog poo, who should walk in through the front door...

"Toki?! Is that you?"

I nearly dropped the smelly surprise on my foot which probably would've been a fitting ending to this day. Horrified, I looked up to see Clark's blithely grinning face peering at me over the front counter. I groaned. My hope of working incognito at Mardi Paws was completely dashed the first day we were open.

"Clark," I grumbled moodily.

My dad looked up from where he was wrestling with a pack of dogs and stood up, wiping his hands on his jeans. His face was a mixture of surprise (probably that anyone actually knew me) and delight (probably assuming, wrongly, that I was doing a good job of acting normal and fitting in enough to have made friends). He went up to the counter to greet Clark as I did my best to fade into the background.

"Toki didn't tell me she had a friend who brought his dog here," my dad chattered, sticking his hand out enthusiastically to shake Clark's hand.

"That's because I don't," I mumbled to myself, slightly feeling the urge to die.

My dad continued warmly, "Jackson Tooley, owner of Mardi Paws."

"Nice to meet you, Mr. Tooley. Clark Kent..."

"Not true!" I warned.

"I'm the proud owner of Simon," Clark finished, pointing to one of the dogs. "I go to school with Toki. We're in some classes together. I was going to take her out for some coffee tonight."

My dad's eyebrows raised, a knowing smile crossing his lips. My slight urge to die now evolved into feeling like I could fall into a black hole and be perfectly content with my fate.

"Got a date already, Toki?" Dad called back, impressed. "Clark, do

I have to give you the overbearing father talk yet? Haha! Just kidding!"
My dad slapped his knees like the redneck he was.

"Please, please stop," I begged, ready to dive straight into a pack of
drooling dogs to escape the horror of the conversation.

"No, sir, not a date. This is all friendly. Trying to get your daughter
better acquainted with the town like a good Buzzer would. I think
Toki has her eye on someone else, someone a little older maybe." Clark
grinned deviously at me from across the room. I resisted every urge in
my body telling me to fling the plastic bag full of dog poop in his face.

"Ah, well, you have excellent timing, it's a little early, but I can handle
the rest from here if you just want to go now, Toki." My dad walked
back to the gang of tail-waggers as I washed my hands, mortified and
wanting the day to end as quickly as possible. "Simon, Simon. Ah! The
noble basset hound!"

Out from the pack pranced the most ridiculous-looking dog in the
whole building (which really was saying a lot). Simon was about half
a dog smaller than the rest and had the build of a hotdog. His floppy
ears bounced all over the place as he trotted toward Clark, tail wagging
happily. A long trail of slime oozed from his mouth wherever he went.

He was happy to see Clark; you didn't need to communicate
with the spirits to tell that much. I never really communicated much
with animal spirits. They had their own ways of communicating be
it through barking, meowing, chirping. It was hard to get a handle
on what they really were trying to say. Most dogs only repeated *Hi,
hello!* 90% of them were only looking for a treat or attention, while the
other 10% made it pretty clear that laying a hand on them was not a
healthy option. Cats weren't any better. They usually just cursed at you
whenever you tried to talk to them.

I clocked out then dejectedly followed Simon and Clark outside. I
froze as soon as I saw him unlock his car.

"You've got to be kidding," I breathed.

"Yup!" Clark beamed as he opened an ancient side door and helped the stubby Simon into the back. "This is it. Isn't she a beauty? She used to be a chicken coop, or at least that's what the guy who sold it to me said."

For lack of a better description, a box on wheels sat in front of us. It was some type of van, I assume, but one that had maybe be unearthed by archaeologists at the turn of the 19th century. It was a bright orange color complete with an ugly purple eagle painted on the hood in painstaking detail.

"This is your car?"

"Well, no," Clark admitted. "It's my van. Hop on in!"

He tried to smoothly open the passenger door for me all gentlemanly-like, but it must have been jammed. He pulled on it, hard, looking at me sheepishly.

"Sorry. This door—tends—to—stick—UGH—in the winter," he said through gritted teeth. The door finally gave way and flew open, nearly knocking him out in the process.

I shook my head as I climbed in. "That shouldn't happen. Are you sure this thing is street legal?"

Clark climbed in the driver's seat and gave the dashboard a happy pat. "It's been legally paid for, and it can drive on a street. Isn't that street legal?"

"No. Not at all." I furtively put my hand on the seat and listened for a moment. This spirit surely had something interesting to say since it had been alive since the time of the dinosaurs.

Buckle up. Please!

It wasn't a polite request. The spirit was actually begging me for my own safety. I don't think I've ever tried to buckle up more tightly than at that moment. I also crossed myself a few times for good luck and looked back at Simon. His tail was wagging, droopy eyes staring at me. I felt a twinge of sympathy. The poor dear probably had no idea the danger he was so obviously in.

Clark grinned at me as he pushed a—*cassette tape*—into the car stereo. "Hope you like Metallica, Tooley. I'll get us to Delta Road in no time. By the way, I've been meaning to tell you, nice shirt…"

"Clark, say anything about it at school, and you will literally be dead by the end of the day."

Chapter Seven: The Crime Scene

IF YOU'RE GOING TO FLY down the road at unadvised speeds in waning light, and if you happen to also be in a death mobile that was seen as a rival when Ford was cranking out Model T's, Metallica is a pretty fitting music choice. Clark belted out the words to "Nothing Else Matters," taking corners at an alarming rate and racing through yellow-turning-red lights. I had to agree with the band at that point. In that van, nothing else save surviving the next second mattered. I couldn't even think about the case or Liam as we flew over potholes and swerved to narrowly miss a row of mailboxes.

"Going a little fast," I called to Clark over the existential chorus.

"I know!" Clark agreed with me, taking a moment to air-guitar an especially important riff. "This song always just flies by when I put it on. Best Metallica song ever! You have great taste in music!"

We were at Delta Road by the end of the song; it was a short ride although I couldn't wait for it to end. I didn't know what I expected Delta Road to look like, but it surprised me how small and unassuming a road it was. Even more unsettling was the fact that I recognized the woods that bordered the road to the west as the same that touched my backyard. How close had Liam and I been the night he died? Was that why I had felt his death through the ground? When I casually asked Clark about the distance, he confirmed my suspicions.

"Yeah, if you live off of Sickles Drive, this so-called crime scene is faster to get to from your house by walking. It's all the winding roads, you know what I mean? You have to drive so slow in this town. Do you know how fast I could go if it were just straight roads? Then again, who wants to walk when you can ride in the Clark-mobile?"

Anybody with a brain stem, I thought to myself as Clark careened onto Delta Road at an alarming rate, forcing me to grab at the seatbelt in a feeble attempt to save myself.

"It isn't a busy road," Clark informed me. "Some of the kids from school live up this way, but there isn't much up there except for some houses."

"Did Liam live out this way?" I asked. I quickly checked behind me to make sure Simon wasn't plastered to the side of the van. He apparently was familiar with his owner's driving habits and had sprawled out across the back seat, tail thumping appreciatively when I made eye-contact with him.

Clark nodded. "Yup. He's got a pretty big house out there. Sydney does, too. They aren't like us townies. Must be quite a life up there, huh? Get whatever you want whenever you want?"

I shrugged. "Liam's not living any life right now, Clark. Can't be all wine and roses."

The van mercifully slowed. We approached a make-shift memorial on the side of the road. I felt a shiver go up my spine as I leapt from the passenger's seat. I stepped away from the van and walked up to a tall evergreen tree that was covered with pictures of Liam, teddy bears, and ribbons.

The tree was humming. It wanted to talk. I glanced back at Clark who was busy trying to get a leash on Simon to take him out. I had a few moments.

I put a hand on the tree and closed my eyes. After a few quiet breaths, it spoke.

Find his phone.

I involuntarily gasped. "His phone?" I repeated in a low voice. I glanced around. Instead of just mourning like the rest of the spirits connected to Liam's death, this one was giving me a directive. That meant that Liam's phone must be around here somewhere. If the spirit sensed it, it must be close. I looked around, dismayed. The side of the road was almost completely overtaken by forest undergrowth as well as fresh piles of snow and ice. Finding Liam's phone from nearly a week ago was going to be impossible.

Clark came over to me. "Well, that was a process," he said, pulling a hat over his unruly hair. "Now that we're here, what's next?"

I took a look down at Simon, who was sniffing around the frozen bushes. Suddenly, an idea sprang to mind. It was something I had never successfully pulled off before, but I was desperate. Unfortunately, there was no way or time to pull the wool over Clark's eyes. The sun was quickly disappearing behind the mountains.

"Clark, I'm going to do something that's going to seem, um… odd. Are you up for it?"

He scratched at his head and regarded me with a questioning look. "Uh, sure. Should I be worried?"

"Only for me," I mumbled as I knelt down, patting my knees to get Simon's attention. The Basset lumbered over to me, tail wagging. I made sure that I didn't touch him, yet. I needed him to listen before he spoke to me. Hopefully he had learned to listen a little better than his owner. I made sure to look into his baleful eyes carefully.

"Simon," I said, "I need some help. I need you to find something that doesn't belong." I placed my hand on the top of his head. "Find something out here that's different."

From behind me, Clark chuckled. "That's not that weird, Toki. I talk to him all the time. Good luck getting him to listen. All he cares about is food and cats."

I locked eyes with him again. His slow tail wag gave me hope.

Hi! He said. *Find different?*

I nodded.

Off like a shot he went, howling for good measure, as he began darting and sniffing around trees in a frenzied state.

I stood up and watched the dog closely, mostly because I didn't know how Clark would respond to the strange scene. Luckily, my companion was never one to let a quiet moment pass for too long.

"Wow. That was amazing! Is that some ancient Japanese technique that your dad taught you to talk to animals? Doggy day care owners know everything!"

I didn't feel like pointing out to Clark that he knew my dad was a simple redneck, far from anything remotely Asian. The less I had to explain, the more normal I could pretend to be. I nodded slightly.

"Just a technique I learned when I was little," I responded.

Clark pranced in the snow beside me happily. "That's so cool! Next time, can you ask him where he hides all my underwear? My stock pile is getting low if you know what I mean…"

It's not that I didn't want to listen to Clark ramble on about his lack of underwear, but something else was nagging at me. Something about this place was unsettling. I felt like ice was spreading through my veins. The sun seemed to be setting faster than normal, and shadows were creeping from the forest with menacing tendrils of darkness. Even the memorial on the side of the road seemed gloomy with wilted flowers, damp stuffed animals, and wind-torn pictures. The spirits, I thought to myself, what was happening to them? I dropped to my knees and placed my hand on the ground.

Gone, gone!

Something was horribly wrong with the spirits. It was as if

they were frozen in fear the moment that Liam died, and all they could remember was his death. They had forgotten themselves and their purpose. I knew the spirits felt and held on to emotions more intensely than we do—that's why it was so easy to understand them. If they lost themselves to grief, only repeating *Gone, gone* forever, would this forest ever heal? If the town were overrun with these despairing spirits, would it ever go back to normal?

"Toki!"

Startled, I jumped up from my daydream. Clark was pointing at snow-covered bushes further into the forest.

"I think Simon has found something."

I saw the wiggling white-and-brown body of the pudgy hound under the thick drooping branches. When he emerged from deep inside the thorny bush, he held something in his slobbery jaws. It was a black cell phone—smeared with a dark red color. I covered my mouth as Simon came trotting up to me, tail drifting back and forth.

I put my hand on his head, and he promptly dropped the cell phone on the ground.

Hi! Different! He exclaimed proudly.

I blew out a breath. "Good boy," I said, scratching at his long ears.

Clark gulped as he bent down to pick up Simon's leash. "Do you think that's Liam's?"

I didn't want to act like I knew for certain. Something like a pit opened up in the bottom of my stomach. The phone had a shattered screen and looked like it had been crushed under something. I tried to turn it on—nothing. When I flipped it over, I noticed the battery was missing.

"I don't know, but it seems like as good a bet as any," I said, picking up the phone carefully to keep any fingerprint evidence that didn't get destroyed by Simon's drool. "Clark, you realize that if this is Liam's phone, this wasn't just any hit-and-run accident. Someone must have thrown the phone into the bushes. That means they were trying to cover up his death."

Clark tilted his head. "Doesn't make any sense. Why not just take the phone with them? Why try to hide it out here?"

I shrugged. He had a point.

"I don't know. I guess I should probably call the police now. They might be able to get trace evidence off this thing and find out why someone wanted to hide it."

Offering me a hand, Clark shook his head. "Good luck with that. No one can get a signal out here. This is a dead zone. Calls drop all the time. We'll have to head back into town to get a signal."

I sighed. That was a predicament. "We should leave the phone here. It's evidence, you know?"

"What if someone really is trying to cover up Liam's death?" Clark pointed out. "They might think twice about leaving it out here and come back for it. Then they might really get rid of it."

Clark was just brimming with insight today. He was right. It was too risky to leave the phone here. Not to mention if I called the police, I'd have to think up an explanation for what Clark and I had been doing on the side of the road near sundown digging around in the bushes. I could only imagine what my parents would infer from the situation. Having to make up so many lies to tell the police and my parents about how I actually found the phone didn't sound too appealing, especially since I might have to also mention the whole breaking-into-a-locker-room incident.

A sudden glimmer of an idea crossed my mind. I wasn't sure what exactly I was doing, but it seemed the only possible next step in my investigation.

Chapter Eight: Rankin

Thursday, February 11th. 12:15 p.m.

CLARK BRAGGED. "Hope you enjoy being a Buzzer the rest of your life, Nichelle. After what I helped Toki do yesterday, she's definitely going to pick me as Best Buzzer. No doubt!" Chewing on his sandwich graciously. he offered me a large wink which I promptly ignored.

Nichelle, grumpy and slouched as far away from us at the table as she could be, scowled in my direction. Apparently, she was still mad at me for trying to solve Liam's murder. I was sure that Clark wasn't exactly helping to smooth things over.

"What happened yesterday?" she asked gruffly.

As Clark was about to respond, I sharply kicked his leg under the table. It didn't feel like the right thing to be spreading around the school. I didn't trust anyone yet, and if someone heard what I found, things could get messy in more ways than one.

Clark yelped. "OW! Um. No. Nothing major happened yesterday. I just helped Toki escape from her job, that's all. Picking up dog poo at her dad's business isn't as glamorous as it sounds."

I sighed. Great cover, Clark. I stabbed pointlessly at a wilted salad with a spork. While Clark and Nichelle began their usual lunchtime war of words, I glanced over at Peter. Silent as ever, he had his eyes glued to the floor.

What was so interesting down there?

Pretending to drop my spork, I leaned down to have a look. I was awestruck. Cellphones were banned from the detention table, so it made sense that Peter was hiding his. The part that didn't make sense was that he didn't just have one; he had two cell phones, one in each hand. From what I could tell, he seemed to be doing something different on each one at the same time. The amount of coordination involved blew my mind. It took my entire concentration just to send out one text.

Wow, I thought. Impressive and slightly obsessive.

As I sat back up, our eyes locked for a moment. Peter stared at me, face as impassive as a stone. It was obvious to see he didn't trust me yet. Did he think I was going to expose his secret or tell on him?

I gave him a quick smile. His secret was safe with me.

He returned his attention back to the phones.

Well, I thought to myself triumphantly, that went well. At least he didn't flip me off.

I yawned and laid my head on my crossed arms. Last night's sleep was even worse than the night before. Getting home after dark raised all sorts of awkward questions with my parents. (Who is this Clark boy? Should we invite him over to dinner one night? What did you do on your 'outing'?) I excused myself from dinner quickly and sealed myself in my room. I had picked up Grandmother's journal, looking for something I had dismissed before.

Rule one, the clock...

"I'm aware!" I shouted, immediately hoping that my dad hadn't heard my outburst. For all he knew, I was acting like a normal girl and had given up getting into arguments with inanimate objects. I ignored the disconcerting fact that the binding white light had appeared again, seeming to tie my hands together with the journal. Digging through the piles of paper in my room, I found the business card that had fallen from the journal when I received it from Grandmother. No more than a blank small rectangular piece of paper, it had a phone number on it— nothing more. No name, no address. There must be a reason for that, I told myself. I tossed the journal across the room in case I found myself permanently tied to it for the rest of my life.

I must have chewed on all ten of my fingernails before I worked up enough courage to dial the number on my cell phone. I prayed to all the spirits everywhere that I was doing the right thing. The phone rang three times before it was picked up on the other end.

"Five o'clock tomorrow evening," a thickly-accented voice on the other line drawled cryptically. "The coffee shop by the hospital. Come alone, and bring the journal."

The hospital? That was on the other side of town. I couldn't even imagine trying to get a ride over there.

"Um," I started sheepishly, "I can't… I don't exactly have a car. Also, I can't drive."

The voice on the other end sighed, exasperated. "You've got to be kiddin' me. What are you, twelve?"

"Hey!" I snapped back into the receiver. "Maybe if you'd like to teach me how to drive a stick-shift, then I could pass the stupid driving test because that's the only type of car my parents like to buy." I also failed to mention that for some reason, manual transmissions were one of the most unpleasant and stubborn spirits to try to communicate with.

The mysterious voice groaned. "Teens," I heard it respond. "Fine, we'll meet somewhere closer for you. In the park across from the high school at four. Do you think you can handle crossing the street on your own without someone holding your hand?"

Oh, this person was going to be a ray of sunshine in my life, I could just tell.

"Yes," I sneered back. "Think you can manage not grumbling about millennials long enough to actually meet me there on time?"

There was a long string of cursing from the other end before the line went dead. Well, it was apparent that whoever was on the other end of the line had been expecting the call. It was a relief to know that whoever it was, he also knew about the journal. Maybe he could take it off of my hands and finish the investigation himself. It probably was a bad move on my part to harass him. This mysterious voice could possibly be the one to shed light on the mystery of who my Grandmother really was.

That night, I dreamt of Grandmother Emi's clock.

Important, it reminded me.

SCHOOL DRAGGED BY slowly after lunch. I kept staring at the school clocks. It was a strange feeling coursing through my body—anxiety and curiosity swirling around each other. When the dismissal bell finally rang, I sprinted to my locker. Time to recheck my backpack. I had packed all the evidence collected so far in separate sandwich bags: the battery-less cell phone, the taped-up note from Liam's athletic locker, the empty prescription bottle, and Grandmother's journal. They looked like little presents waiting to be handed out at Christmas time. It would be a huge relief to get rid of everything into some more capable hands. This investigation was taking a hard toll on my sleep schedule.

I started walking down the deserted hallways when I heard a girl's desperate sounding voice.

"...and now you act like nothing ever happened! You don't return my texts or calls, you completely ignored me in the halls. I can't take it. Do you realize everything that I did for you, Mike?"

Mike? Could it be Mike Treverly? I slowed my walk and quietly stopped, hidden behind a row of nearby lockers.

"Yeah, Ashley, I know what you did, all right? I was there. Calm down, will you?" A gruff voice replied back, seemingly annoyed.

The girl snapped back, "No! I'm not going to calm down. I tried to get into his locker the other day. I had to snap off the lock; I think someone has been in there. It was all gone. Everything. I don't know if the janitors cleaned it out, or if the police..."

"Shhh! Shut-up! It's not the police, got it? Don't you know anything? They'd have to get a search warrant and tell us they are searching our lockers. Rossi's not going to let that happen on his watch. He doesn't exactly have a choice, if you know what I mean. I'm sure it was just the janitors. They have to clean it out when people die. Can't just leave it sitting there forever."

"That's awful," the girl replied, voice tinged with tears. "You... you used me."

I could almost hear the shrug of meaty shoulders as Mike replied, "Dunno. Maybe you let yourself be used. We had our fun, right? But things are just complicated now. I need a break. State's in two weeks, and I'm kinda stressed out. Give me some space."

There was a moment of silence. The tension was so thick you had to scoop your way out of it.

"Next time do your own dirty work and leave me out of it. Screw you, Mike."

I heard the stomping of feet off in the other direction. I peeked around the lockers to see the back of a girl with a dark pixie haircut storm toward the front doors. She was followed by the giant form of Mike Treverly as he leisurely strolled toward the parking lot, whistling a self-assured tune.

Something twisted in my stomach. Why did it seem like everyone was more concerned about themselves than what actually happened to Liam? I checked my phone—4:05. I was going to be late to meet my contact. I exited out a side door and ran across the road toward the park.

It wasn't hard to spot the mysterious man. Considering that it felt like negative 40 degrees outside, there were only two people stupid enough to be hanging out in a park. I saw a strangely familiar older man with blonde hair and piercing blue eyes. His hands were pushed deeply into his pockets, and his very essence seeped with grumpiness.

I approached him hesitantly, unsure of how to start this strange conversation about murder cover-ups. He looked up at me sharply and wiped at his nose with a thick glove.

"It's nearly a quarter past. Don't you know how to tell time, or have they even taught that to you in kindergarten yet?"

Any slight bit of doubt I had that this was the same person from the phone call last night was erased.

My teeth chattered. "I'm sorry. My foot froze to the sidewalk on the way over. I was just following the advice of the genius who thought it was a great idea to meet outside in a polar vortex."

After enduring a swath of cursing that would've made a sailor take notes, the man stood up hastily and jerked a thumb over to the parking lot. "Fine, fine. Have it your way. Little baby divas can't handle normal winter weather. Where'd you come from anyway kid? Hawaii?"

"Oregon," I replied sulkily as I followed him. "Don't worry. We had cantankerous old guys like you there too, so I'm used to…" I stopped as soon as I saw him unlock his car door. "Oh, this is just my luck."

Yes, apparently my cheerful counterpart was none other than the sheriff of the town himself. He climbed into the familiar squad car that I saw patrolling the street every day. Good job, Tooley, I reprimanded myself. I had been mouthing off enough to get arrested and put away for the rest of my high school career.

"Get in before I change my mind," he ordered.

I slid in the passenger's seat, immediately blasted in the face by two air vents pouring out lukewarm air. My nose defrosted and started running like it was in a marathon. I dabbed at it carefully with a tissue.

"I'm Sheriff Rankin," he announced, turning the radio down.

"Yeah, I know. I pass by your reelection billboard all the time. Um… it doesn't exactly seem like reelection season though."

Rankin barked out something that sounded like a harsh laugh. "I leave that thing up all the time. I've been sheriff here before you were potty-trained. That sign makes people think that I'm the most qualified guy out here for the job, you know? Maybe my job is some sort of hot position that people are just itchin' to get in. Truth is, I've run unopposed every time. Nobody really wants to be sheriff in a town with no real crime. Drunk driving, noise complaints, that's about all I deal with." He thought about it for a moment, then added in a strange voice, "Hasn't been a murder here in this town for about ten years."

So I had heard before. Why then exactly was his number in Grandmother's journal? I took a closer look at him. It suddenly hit me. There was a reason he looked familiar, and it wasn't just from his billboard.

"The assisted living home!" I remembered. "You were there when… when…"

"When she gave you the journal and passed her responsibilities to you? Yeah, that was me. Who do you think dragged you back to the chair and put the journal in your pocket when it was all over?"

I stopped, shaking my head. "Passed her responsibilities? What do you mean?"

"You have the journal with you?"

I nodded and pulled it out. It dutifully began reciting the list of rules to me again as soon as I touched it. I watched with unease as the white line began crossing over my wrists again.

"See that white light?" the sheriff asked.

I was mystified. "You see it too? You know what it is, then!"

The sheriff shook his head. "No, sorry kid. I don't see it. It's too weak right now, apparently. If you get further in your investigation, the light will get easier for normal people like me to see. Your grandmother told me it looks like some sort of white light running around your arm? It's the spirit of the journal trying to bind with you. It won't go away until you outright refuse it or accept it."

That was something new. I had never seen a spirit before; I had only heard them. Suddenly, the white light didn't seem as threatening as it had before. It wound around my wrists tentatively, almost as if it were waiting for something while the journal kept reciting the rules in the background. *Rule four: Only those who approach the light...*

"Why can I see this spirit?" I asked, putting the journal down so I could concentrate. "I've been talking to spirits all of my life, but I've never seen one."

The sheriff shrugged. "There's lots of things I don't know, kid. Take the way that your Grandmother talks to spirits. One day she comes up to me telling me that she can help me solve the murder of this girl. That was a long time ago. At first I thought she was crazy—going around and talkin' to houses and trees. Then she starts figuring out all sorts of things that seem impossible to understand. Finally, I start believin' that maybe it's all real. Those spirits don't talk to me, though. Only to her. When I asked her if she ever saw spirits, she told me no, except that she sees the spirit of this journal because it's so strong. It has to be."

If I thought I was going to clear up any confusion, I was dreadfully wrong. "It has to be a strong spirit? Why?"

I could feel hesitation from the sheriff as if he didn't really want to tell me the next part.

"This place, kid. Devil's Ford. Weird name, right? When the town was first founded, bad things happened right from the beginning. The murder rate was off the charts. People would just up and disappear for years until their bones were found years later. Everyone got mean and nasty and acted without any impulse control. It was a miserable place to live before your Grandmother got here. You know it's colder here year-round than any other place in Colorado? Why do you think that is?"

I considered it for a moment, remembering back to the place where Liam had died. "It's the spirits," I guessed. "It seems like they're terrified of something. They don't act like any other spirits I've known before."

Impressed, Rankin nodded his head. "That's exactly what your grandmother told me. She told me that there's something really dark here. Something like an ancient curse that's settled around the town. Whatever it does, it affects everyone—people, animals, rocks, trees. It spreads like a dark wildfire and infects things. When someone is taken by that infection, part of this place dies. It gets colder. People start to become hopeless."

I had heard stories of evil spirits before, but I had never encountered one. I honestly thought that they were fairy tales meant to scare people or exaggerations. Sure, there were spirits who were snobby or just plain aggressive and violent, but an evil spirit intent on destroying an entire town? That was beyond my realm of experience. I was skeptical.

"Why do people stay here?" I asked.

"Well, the short answer is your Grandmother moved here about fifty years ago. She started changin' things. The people here don't even know what's goin' on around them. I mean, they know that they feel cold and depressed, but they don't think anything of it. Most of the time, your grandmother fixes things so that they get back to normal. That's why she's our Protector. Now that she's sick, we're in a real bad place. There's no way to fix what's wrong if she can't do her job. That's why she wanted to give her responsibilities—her abilities—to you. You can talk to spirits, just like she can. Your Grandmother was hopin' maybe you could be the next Protector—if you accepted, that is." He sighed and rubbed at his face, regarding me out of the corner of his eyes. "I sure hope she knows what she was doing. Little pissant like you wouldn't have been my first choice. Don't you have an older brother or something? Maybe he would be more qualified."

I was offended. "Please. Ken doesn't know how to talk to things without dating them first. And what exactly is a pissant?"

"That's not important now. At least tell me—is your Grandmother right? Can you… talk to spirits, too?"

I paused for a moment. This was my new start, my dad had told me. My moment to be a normal person. If I told the truth, that moment of normalcy would be out of my grasp forever.

The sheriff waited for my answer with piercing eyes. A light snow had begun to fall outside.

I finally nodded.

"Prove it," the sheriff said, unconvinced. "Tell me what my car says."

I tentatively put my gloved hands on the car and listened for a moment. Its response was three sharply punctuated curse words which if I ever repeated would probably land me lunch detention for the rest of my life.

I looked back at him, appalled. "Do you kiss your mother with that mouth?"

For the first time since we met, the sheriff looked relieved. "You're the real deal, eh? Finally, we get a bit of luck on our side. Well, now that we've got that all figured out, it's time for you and I to start working together."

"You need my help?" I asked with a chuckle. "Did Grandmother do your whole job for you or something?"

I thought the comment might set him off, but then Rankin made this face that made think I was closer to the truth than I realized.

"Yeah," he replied. "Like I said, no unnatural deaths in this town until last week."

"Liam."

Rankin looked over at me sharply. "Do you know what happened?"

"Not a lot," I admitted, "but since you're supposedly the sheriff around here, I have some stuff I think you should see."

"You've been snooping around already?" Rankin asked, sounding somewhat impressed. "Then you definitely have your grandmother's blood. All right. Tell me everything."

Chapter Nine: The Protector

I DID TELL HIM EVERYTHING. All of the events of the past few days came gushing out so easily as if the bits and pieces I had been collecting needed to be released in a giant blob. Figuring I had nothing to lose, I even left in the parts about talking to the spirits in the locker room and the roadside where Liam had died. Rankin didn't even bat an eye when I told him about how the spirits had led me to the suspension letter, the empty vodka bottle, and the broken cell phone.

Instead, he listened. For someone who had spent most of her life listening to others, I was relieved. Not only did he listen, nothing sounded crazy to him. It was as if he had done this a hundred times before. When I told him that, he let out his characteristic short barking laugh.

"A hundred times? Yeah, you could say that," he said, eyes twinkling as he drew a hand over his grizzled face. "So you think that Paxton's death is a cover-up. I suppose you guess that the cell phone proves that. Someone may be sweatin' pretty badly over the fact you found that."

"If only we can figure out what's on it," I said, frustrated. "Can you send it to a crime lab or something? Maybe they can get into it and find out why someone would try to make sure it wasn't found."

For a moment, Rankin looked pained. He started the car up. For the first time in our conversation, he looked uncertain of what to say.

"I don't think you'll have time for that," he finally responded.

I blinked. "What? What do you mean?"

"I don't understand it all," Rankin admitted sheepishly as he pulled out from the parking lot and began creeping down the road. "Your grandmother would explain parts of it to me, but other parts may have been too hard for me to comprehend without talking to the spirits myself. Devil's Ford was a nightmare of a town until Emi came along. Tell me—why do you think the murders and unnatural deaths suddenly stopped fifty years ago?"

"Maybe it was the invention of moving pictures," I suggested casually. "It probably gave something for people to do around here."

Rankin ignored my flippant comment. "Think about it, kid. Maybe the murders and the deaths didn't stop. Hear me out. Murders do still happen here. They happen here all the time, more than normal, just like back fifty years ago. As long as I've been an officer, your grandmother has worked her back off trying to solve these murders. She uses that journal there to put all the clues together, and eventually she figures out what happened."

I opened the journal again, flipping through the pages and pages of old notes. Most had that strange shimmering embossed mark.

"These are all murders that she had solved before?"

Rankin nodded at me as he turned on to my street. He seemed to know where I lived. I figured it was the sheriff's job to know exactly what house the new families in a tiny town had moved into.

I squinted at the pages. "Interesting. Some of the cases have a dark red stamp. Why do they look different?"

Rankin was deep in thought. "They weren't solved in time, or they just weren't solved, period."

"So, what, I've got a time limit or something to solve the crime?"

He glanced at me. "Your grandmother told me there was no way you could miss the journal's rules. Think about what they are."

Rule one: the clock is both your enemy and your friend.

Oh, I thought to myself. Now it makes sense.

"What happens if I don't solve the crime in time?" I asked.

Rankin sighed. "Emi told me this all the time. She used to say, 'The past remains the past, the future becomes the present.'"

I scoffed. "Where did she get that line from, a fortune cookie? Was she always this cryptic?"

Rankin pulled up in front of my house. I could feel that he wanted to tell me more but was holding back. It was infuriating, like getting only half of the answers back on a test.

"Look kid, I promised your grandmother that I wouldn't go spillin' everything at once. She insisted that some of the stuff you had to figure out for yourself, or else I might scare you away for good. All I can say is do whatever you can to solve this crime. Break laws for all I care. Listen to your head, your heart, the journal, and most importantly, the spirits. Your grandmother is the kindest, smartest woman I've ever known. If you've got half of what she's got, you'll understand soon enough. It's up to you now, not me." He handed me back my bag of evidence. "Prove that you're not a complete waste of space, okay?"

I rolled my eyes. "Wow, great motivational speech there, Sheriff. You know, I think it's so novel of you to go against the whole 'jaded and grizzled cop' stereotype."

Rankin snorted at me. "Tell you what. You solve this crime, and I'll go by your school and personally let your principal know what a shiny, upstandin' citizen you are. That'll get you out of homework for at least three weeks, I reckon."

"Hmmm. Deal," I agreed. Not so much because I cared about doing the homework, but the thought of the cantankerous sheriff having to give me any sort of public compliment would be reward enough in itself.

"Before you go… here. Your grandmother asked me to give this to you at the right time. I don't really know what the 'right time' is, so I figure this is as good enough a time as any."

He got out of the car and went into his trunk for a moment. When he came back, he pushed a big box at me.

I struggled to climb out of the car with the giant box just as the sun disappeared. He rolled down the passenger window to bark one more order at me.

"Remember, you can't be dilly-dallying around. There's a lot riding on this. You screw this up, just know—there are no second chances for anyone."

I awkwardly waved him off with one hand, tired of his doom-and-gloom attitude. "Great, thanks for the advice. Look, I think there's a cat stuck in a tree somewhere. You should probably go and do your job now."

With a string of fresh curses I'd never been called before in my life, the sheriff gave me a very special glare and peeled off.

I sighed and carefully dropped the box to rub at my temples, trying to think for a moment. I didn't want to go inside the house yet. I needed to process everything that had happened. Hauling the box with me, I tromped around the side of the house, ignoring the snow that was falling in thick clumps around me. I headed over toward my newly acquainted boulder in the back. Wiping the snow off of it carefully, I sat down and pressed my hands against the rock.

Different? The rock asked, concerned.

I nodded sadly. "Yeah. Everything's different. I can feel it." I shivered and looked around. It felt like I was being watched. "I don't even know where to start, to tell you the truth. I'm supposed to put all this evidence together in a shorter amount of time than a real detective would have. I don't even know why I'm supposed to, either. It's not like it's going to bring him back or anything."

82

There was a swirling sensation around my body as I sat there, and I shuddered. It felt like there was a thirty degree drop in just a moment. I had an eerie feeling like someone had just stepped next to me, but when I turned around I saw nothing. I closed my eyes for a second. Try to focus on the darkness, I told myself. If it is an evil spirit, like Sheriff Rankin predicted, shouldn't I be able to communicate with it somehow? I pressed my fingers into the snow beside the rock and took a breath.

"What do you want?" I murmured, trying to force all my concentration into the ground. "Talk to me."

For a moment, in my mind, I got a glimpse of a figure. It reached its hand out and touched my shoulder gently. In an instant, my whole body went numb. I felt every neuron in my brain popping as a dark light swirled around me. The breath left my body; I felt like I was being pressed from the outside like a crushed soda can. It was too much to take.

"Stop!" I cried, tearing myself away from the figure. I flew off of the rock backward into the snow, hitting my head against the frozen ground.

Taking in deep breaths of air, I stared up into the cloudy night sky, flakes of snow falling on my face gently. What in the world was that? Was that the evil spirit? It seemed doubtful. Whatever that figure was, it didn't seem like it intended to hurt me. It was trying to reach out to me. Whatever had happened to me didn't seem malicious, but it certainly did seem dangerous.

I heard a rattle from the backyard next to me and put my head up.

Imagine my shock to see Peter from the detention table dragging garbage bags behind him to the trash cans by the side of his house. He glanced over into my yard and saw me sprawled on the powdery ground as if I were in the middle of making a snow angel.

"Peter?" I asked, standing up and brushing snow off of my pants.

"You live here?"

He didn't respond.

"Yeah okay, stupid question," I admitted. "It's not like you'd be taking out a stranger's trash. It's just I've never seen you here before. So... I guess we're neighbors?"

Something audibly buzzed and lit up the pockets of his jacket. He looked a little impatient as if sitting in the freezing weather next to a rancid garbage can talking to a crazy new kid wasn't exactly where he wanted to be.

That's when an idea suddenly popped into my brain.

"Peter, I have a favor to ask..." I began, fully expecting to be flipped off just for asking.

He glanced at me impassively as I dug through my bag of evidence.

I held up my sandwich bag with the bloody cell phone. "Look, this is going to sound weird. This is Liam Paxton's phone. I found it hidden around where he was killed. I'm not sure why it was there, but it seems like someone really didn't want it to be found or traced."

I detected a spark of interest crossing Peter's face as he listened.

I continued, "I need to find out why someone didn't want this phone found. As you can see, the screen's all cracked and there's no battery. It's probably password protected, too. Would you possibly consider hacking into it for me?"

His eyes lit up with a type of mischievousness that I'd never associated with the usually expressionless Peter. I suppose the word "hacking" did the job of breaking through his wall. I extended my arm with the sandwich bag like an offering. After curiously studying the bloody phone, Peter plucked it from my reach and stuck it in his pocket. He nodded at me.

I grinned at him. "Thanks. Now you're definitely in the running with Nichelle and Clark to get sprung from the detention table. Um, not to be pushy, but I need that as soon as possible."

He nodded again. I turned to grab the box and head into my house. "Toki?"

His voice was calm and clear. I turned and looked at him. He looked almost as surprised as I did; we were having a conversation.

"Yes?" I asked hesitantly.

He paused for a moment. "You… talk to things, don't you? And you listen to them. I was watching you from my window." He nodded to the rock that I had been sitting on.

Well, that explained that eerie feeling earlier of being watched. I swallowed. It seemed like it was pointless to hide it now, especially since Peter was actually talking to me.

My face grew red. "Yeah," I admitted.

Peter nodded, surprisingly cool. "My grandfather was the same way. He used to talk to our house, and our garden and vegetables. He told me everything the squash and tomatoes said…" His voice trailed off as he stared at a corner of his backyard that had small pickets and chicken wire around it. With a quiet voice, Peter said, "I miss him."

Involuntarily, tears welled up in my eyes. I tried to hold them in— if I cried out here, the tears would for sure freeze to my face. "I'm so sorry, Peter."

Peter glanced back at me, face grim. "Thank you. I didn't mean to embarrass you, but when I saw you out here talking, it just brought back a lot of memories." He smiled very slightly. "Good ones."

I heaved a sigh of relief. "Good, so you don't think I'm weird then?"

He gave me a side-eye. "No, you are certainly weird, Toki. It's not necessarily a bad thing, you know." With a small wave he added, "I'll get to work on this phone. See you tomorrow?"

"Of course," I answered, hauling the large box back in my arms. "Thank you, Peter."

I finally came back into the house and went straight into my room. I put the box down on my bed and regarded it curiously. It came from

Grandmother Emi. What could it be?

As I opened the flaps, a very audible humming filled the room. I groaned as I pulled out the clock from grandmother's bedside table.

Important! It chirped at me as soon as I touched it.

I nodded slowly. "I remember," I said, clearing off a space on my dresser to put it on. What a strange gift, I thought to myself. Seems just like a regular clock. However, the more I looked at it, the more I realized there was something very wrong with it.

There was a small plate within the face that told the day and date, and it was ridiculously wrong. My phone clearly read that today was Thursday, February 11th. The face of grandmother's clock, however, insisted that it was Friday, February 5th.

I frowned. "You're broken," I informed the clock as I laid my hand down on it.

Important!

I couldn't imagine why grandmother would so specifically instruct Sheriff Rankin to give me a busted clock that had nothing more insightful to say than *Important!* I shook my head and eyed it suspiciously. Maybe once Peter had figured out Liam's phone, he could take a look at this clock.

"Toki? Is everything all right? You haven't touched your dinner."

I looked up from my plate of mashed potatoes that I had been swirling into something that could've been made by Jackson Pollock. My mom looked at me from behind her perfectly coifed curtain of dark hair, eyebrows raised in concern. I managed a weak and thoroughly unconvincing smile.

"Yeah Mom. I'm fine. Just, um, overwhelmed with everything."

That was the understatement of the year. Between being thrust into a completely different curriculum at school, trying to understand the labyrinth hallway design at Chamberlain High School, helping

86

Dad at Mardi Paws, trying to find all my stuff which was scattered in at least forty different boxes around the house and now also having the responsibility of solving some kid's death, I had forgotten who I used to be. My past life seemed so far away now. I missed simple talks on the beach with my driftwood friend.

Mom tilted her head at me. "Anything I can help with? Would any of this be related to a certain Clark Kent that I've been hearing about?"

"Ugh. No. He's the least of my problems. Whatever Dad's been telling you about him, you can pretty much ignore it. That includes his name."

"Well things can't be that bad, Toki. At least you're making friends, right?"

I didn't know how to respond to that. Nichelle, Clark, and Peter— they weren't actually friends, were they? They were using me to get out of detention, and I was using them to solve a mystery. That didn't seem like much of a basis for a deep and lasting friendship.

I shrugged.

Mom pursed her lips. I could tell that she felt badly that she couldn't solve my problems. Maybe she blamed herself for uprooting the family for Grandmother Emi. I didn't blame her for any of that. I would do the same for her, too. Our relationship, however, felt different from theirs. There was so much there I didn't understand, like a giant wall that had been built up year after year of separation. It made me a little nervous but more curious than ever. What had happened between my mom and grandmother to cause such a rift?

I forced a smile. "I think I'm just tired. Hey, next time that you visit Grandmother, can I go with you? I'd really like to see her again."

Taken aback, my mom nodded. "Sure. We can go see her this weekend if you'd like."

I excused myself from the table and threw the paper plate away in the trash. Our real dinner plates were still missing somewhere within the horde of boxes. I went to my room and pulled out the journal, ignoring the rules being read to me dutifully once again.

I took a pen from my backpack and tapped it on the pages, thinking. If this was now my case to solve, I needed to add my own notes to it. If I organized my thoughts, maybe I'd discover something I'd overlooked before.

Coach Rossi—might have accidentally hit Liam, drunk driving?
Seems to "owe" something to Treverly.
Mike Treverly—pompous jerk. Thinks pretty highly of himself.
Used Ashley then dumped her. For what purpose, though?
Ashley-what's-her-face—Did something for Mike. Broke into
Liam's athletic locker after we did. What was she looking for?

Something tied all of these people together. Supposedly they were all at the wrestling meet the night that Liam died. There must have been something that happened to set all of the events in motion. I had to figure out the common thread.

The question was how could I go back into the past to piece everything together? I was trying to pry into all the details of someone's life who I didn't even know.

That night, I couldn't sleep. Whenever I closed my eyes I could hear the ticking of Grandmother's clock getting louder and louder. When I opened my eyes, the clock's face seemed to glow, staring at me insistently. *February 5th*, it said plainly.

I slipped into a fitful sleep. When I woke at two in the morning, I looked over at the clock.

February 4th, it told me.

Chapter Ten: Wrong

Friday, February 12th. 7:20 a.m.

I STUFFED MY HANDS deeply in my winter coat as my teeth chattered. Besides maybe getting a total of one hour of sleep last night, I couldn't seem to warm myself up. Ever since being touched by the dark spirit last night, I felt like a biting wind was following me everywhere I went. Everything, from the tip of my nose to the bottoms of my feet, felt frigid. It felt like if I breathed the air too deeply, my brain would freeze. The school was open to the students, but I didn't dare go inside yet. I had a plan.

I finally saw Ashley come in from the parking lot at 7:30. I first noticed her trademark pixie hair as she exited from a beige four-door sedan. I felt a moment of jealousy. Wouldn't it be so much more convenient for everyone if I had my own car? That wouldn't happen until I finally overcame my phobia and decided to learn how to drive a stick-shift. I wondered for a moment what kind of offerings a manual transmission would appreciate. Some coolant, maybe? Or something pricier like a high-end oil change?

I quickly made my way over to the girl. "Um, hi! Ashley, right?" I asked, putting on my best friendly and innocent façade. If this plan was going to work, I had to commit and ham it up.

Looking surprised, Ashley blinked at me, trying to place a name to my face. "Uh, yeah. You are...?"

"Toki Tooley. I'm new here."

"Oh," a small smile passed through Ashley's face. I couldn't tell if she was trying to be friendly or just found my name to be ridiculous. "Hi. What's up?"

"Well," I said, preparing a lie so big that if it backfired on me, I'd be labeled a psychopath, "you see, ever since I started school here, um.... This is really awkward. There's this kid that's been following me around. I gave him my number one day because I was just trying to be friendly, but it seems like he's being really flirty."

"Okay..." Ashley said, frowning.

I modestly tucked a strand of hair behind my ear, prepared to tell the biggest lie of them all. I was very glad Nichelle wasn't around to hear me, or I was likely to get punched.

"Well, the thing is, I think this kid is kinda cute. But I don't know anything around here. I don't want to step on anyone's toes, you know? I asked one of those detention kids about him, and she told me that you were kind of a thing with him. If he is with you, I don't want to..."

Ashley stopped cold, her face turning into a mix of realization, disgust, and sadness. "Wait, don't tell me. Is it Mike Treverly?"

I nodded.

She let out an exasperated sigh and shook her head. "Look, Toki, the best advice I can give you is to stay far away from him. That's not because I'm with him, trust me, I'm done with that. You seem like a nice person. Unfortunately, Mike is not. He has some real self-esteem issues, no matter how big his head might seem."

I frowned, trying to look confused. "What do you mean? I thought I heard that he's the best wrestler in school."

"He is now."

We walked into the hallway of the school. A few students were milling around, eating their breakfasts on the floor or listening to music on their phones. Some were outright napping on the linoleum. I caught a glimpse of Mike. He was talking to Sydney. She stood at her open locker, shaking her head in a daze at something as Mike spoke to her. They both look flustered.

"See?" Ashley said, pointing to him. "Look at that. He's always looking for someone else to inflate his ego. You probably don't know since you're new, but Sydney's boyfriend just died a week ago. Mike was his best friend, and now he's trying to hook up with her. What kind of person does that?"

I watched the two carefully. Mike leaned closer to Sydney, talking to her in intense hushed whispers. Sydney was staring into her locker blankly, chewing on her fingernails.

"How do you know that he's trying to hook up with her?" I asked.

Ashley rolled her eyes, throwing a look of disgust at both of them. "Because that's what he does. Mike's never been happy with just being himself. He was always comparing himself to Liam—that kid who died. It's all he would ever talk about. It almost seemed like he was obsessed with beating Liam at something. I was the wrestling manager, so I saw them both a lot. Mike always got angry that Liam was better than him. I was stupid enough to listen to him as long as I did." She turned to me. "Toki, I mean it. That kid is not worth your time. There's something really not right with him, and if the death of his best friend didn't change that, nothing will."

With that, she spun around and marched away, unable to take the sight of Mike and Sydney together. I continued to inconspicuously watch the two. Mike had pulled something out of his pocket and was hiding it in his meaty hand. He talked to Sydney earnestly. He gently took her hand, slipping the mysterious object into hers, and leaned closer, whispering something. For a moment, I thought Ashley might be right. Maybe these two were trying to hook up.

Sydney suddenly broke from her daze and looked up at Mike angrily. She threw whatever he had handed to her into her locker with a great racket and slammed the door, nearly taking off Mike's head in the process. She marched away after giving him a disgusted look. He followed her closely, pleading for her to stop.

I watched them disappear down the hallway then quietly praised my luck. Sydney's blow-up had left me an opening if I could act fast enough. I walked over to her locker, thankful that it was still early enough that the hallways were almost empty. Because she had stormed off, she hadn't spun the combination to reset the lock on her door. She had practically left it open for me to snoop.

I gently lifted the handle of the locker; it welcomed me in. I had to work quickly. A scan of the locker filled me with sudden disgust. If there was anything that really pushed my buttons, it was a hoarder. All of those beautiful spirits of objects just sitting around and growing dust, not being used the way they were meant to—something about that just bothered me. Not only that, but spirits in hoarded places became frantic and difficult to reason with. They usually yelled whenever you talked to them, desperate to get some kind of positive attention. This locker was one of my worst nightmares.

Sydney, it seemed, was a closet hoarder. I searched through the bottom pile of waste. Crumpled pieces of assignments that all looked like they had been in a battle with a red pen *(Study harder!)*, three empty Starbucks coffee cups *(Recycle, please)*, a water-stained notebook *(Useless, useless)*, three empty bottles of blue fingernail polish *(Wrong!)*, a dirty winter glove *(Friend?)*, and some used tissues *(Unsanitary!)* screamed at me as I ransacked through them.

None of the trash was what I was really looking for, so I held back a gag and stuck my hand deeper into the pile, digging furiously as more spirits shouted at me in a bid to get noticed. Finally, I heard it. As soon as my hand touched the cool metal lid, I heard them chant together.

Use as directed!

"Bingo," I whispered, pulling out a small mint tin and shoving it into my pocket. From our conversation, I knew these weren't any ordinary mints. I didn't even have to look inside to understand that Mike had handed Sydney a box full of illegal prescription pills.

The theory that Liam had been set up and betrayed by his best friend was becoming stronger by the minute. Something twisted in the bottom of my stomach as I walked away. No wonder I had always preferred my spirits to human friends. What kind of person could do this to another and just act like everything was fine?

I SAT AT THE LUNCH TABLE silently, slightly apart from the other two. Peter wasn't there. The mint tin was burning a hole in my pocket. My eyes felt raw and were probably puffy and dark from the lack of sleep. My hair was frizzy and almost a constant mess because I couldn't go anywhere without my hat; I was constantly freezing. I was still trying to process what had happened this morning, and seeing Mike Treverly bounce around the cafeteria without a care in the world was making me physically ill. I stared glumly at the table ahead of me, lost.

Nichelle and Clark must have immediately sensed my mood. For the first time, they weren't arguing with each other. They sat silently, glancing at me from time to time and sharing a worried look with each other.

"Toki," Nichelle started, her voice always like a knife, "don't you think you're taking this a little too seriously? It's not your job to find out who killed him, you know. We do have a sheriff out here that's pretty good at solving all the crimes."

I didn't respond. It would've taken too much energy to explain how Sheriff Rankin had debunked that theory pretty quickly.

Nichelle stared at me for a moment, then continued. "By the way, Clark and I have a question for you."

I sighed, putting my head down into my arms. "This isn't a good time," I mumbled.

I could hear Clark scoot closer to me on the bench. "Well, it's just that Nichelle and I have been talking, and we have both noticed something... um... different about you."

Well, this should be interesting. I raised my head slightly and looked at the two of them. "You have?"

Nichelle tapped her foot impatiently. "Yeah. Like the whole thing with cleaning the trash can and then randomly finding the vodka bottle? What on earth possessed you to do that? How did you know something was in there?"

"Also," Clark added, "the whole thing with you talking to my dog. He never pays any attention to me, but you talk to him for two seconds, and suddenly he does exactly what you told him to. I mean that was super cool, but it was also kinda weird."

I lowered my head again. Great job acting normal, Toki. The kids here figured you out in a record five days. Time to prepare myself for the jokes, the looks, the whispers, the eventual shunning.

I heard an impatient sigh. "Put your head up, girl. Clark and I know something's going on."

"We're your friends. Don't you trust us?" The voice next to me asked a little sadly.

I pondered that question for a moment. Did I trust them? Here they were, asking me to divulge my biggest secret. How were they going to react? Visions of the first day of kindergarten flew through my head again. If I let my secret out, more hurtful things than crayons could certainly be lobbed at me. It honestly didn't seem worth the risk. Hadn't I made a half-hearted promise to my dad that I would try my best to be normal?

Maybe that was the key to everything, though. I wasn't normal. Normal people didn't talk to the spirits, and normal people didn't go hunting down killers in small towns at the behest of their grandmothers. Normal people also didn't go around driving hideous reformed chicken coops and pretending to be the alter-ego of Superman. They didn't go breaking into locker rooms and picking fights with anyone who looked at them the wrong way. Normal people certainly couldn't control two phones at once or hack the school network.

No, I wasn't normal. Luckily for me no one else at this table seemed to be normal, either.

I sat up and took a deep breath. Clark and Nichelle watched me wordlessly.

How to start? I suppose the only way was to show them. Trying to explain it would just make it more unbelievable. I looked over at Clark.

"Give me your necklace," I said, gesturing to the guitar pick on the silver chain he wore every day.

Clark hesitated for a moment, which made me even more sure that this was a good start. The guitar pick obviously meant something to him which would make whatever it said more convincing that I wasn't just making this all up.

"What are you going to do?" He asked nervously as he handed it over. "Be careful—that's the first guitar pick I ever owned."

I ignored his question and held the pick in the palm of my hand. I closed my eyes for a moment and rubbed it with my thumb.

Waking, it murmured dreamily.

I looked up at Clark and handed the necklace back. "It said, 'Waking.'"

The color immediately drained from his face, and he stared at me wordlessly. I knew I had hit the nail on the head, even if I had no idea what the word itself meant to him. Nichelle looked at him expectantly.

"Waking? What's that?"

It took Clark a minute to find his words as he stared at the pick. I could see his eyes glaze over in fond memories, and finally a smile appeared. He looked up at me, seemingly impressed and joyful.

"'Waking' was the first song I ever wrote. I think I was thirteen. I wrote it on my first guitar with this pick." He shook his head in wonder. "There's no way you could've known that. Did it say anything else?"

"No. Usually it's only a few words, three if you're lucky." Or, I failed to mention, if you were unlucky, it would repeat the same set of rules at you over and over, but this didn't seem like the time to mention Grandmother's journal.

Nichelle, skeptical as always, tapped her fingers against her arm. "You could've figured that out somehow," she said. "Clark talks non-stop. He's probably told everyone the name of that song at some point."

I shrugged. "Okay, let's try something from you."

Nichelle regarded me for a moment before digging into her backpack. She pulled out a piece of red cloth that was wound up neatly into a ball and placed it into my hands. "Here."

I stared, trying to figure out what it was. It looked like a long bandage with Velcro to fasten the ends together. I listened for a moment. This spirit took a little longer than Clark's guitar pick to speak, but figuring that it was Nichelle's that made perfect sense to me.

I heard the word and frowned.

"Raptor?" I asked, unsure if I had heard it correctly.

One look at Nichelle's face told me I was correct. Her mouth hung open.

"How the heck did you..." she trailed off for a moment. Finally, she took a deep breath as she grabbed the bandage back from me. "These are my gym wraps for kickboxing. My fighter name is 'Raptor'. That's what everyone there knows me by."

I nodded. "Makes sense, then."

Clark was grabbing his hair in an attempt to make his head

understand. "I don't get it. How do you do it? Are you some sort of magician or psychic?"

I sighed. Time to really test how open-minded these two were.

"There are spirits everywhere," I began. "Every object, person, and animal has some sort of spirit. I've been talking to them ever since I was little. I think my mom used to, and my grandmother still does. I listen to them, and they speak to me. Sometimes you need to give them a little TLC to get them to speak, like the trash can in the locker room," I said, nodding to Nichelle.

She sat down heavily, trying to understand what I was saying. "Okay, so why are you the only one who hears them? Why haven't I ever heard one before?"

"You probably have but you've never realized it. I mean, think about it. Just because you don't speak to them the same way I do doesn't mean you haven't heard them. Clark, haven't you ever written a song that seemed like you had known it your whole life? Doesn't your guitar feel like it's a part of you sometime?"

Clark nodded slowly. "Yeah, you're right. Sometimes I hear what I'm playing, and I don't even realize it's me."

I turned to Nichelle. "When you go kickboxing, can't you read the movements of your opponent without thinking about it? Dodging, kicking, punching—it must feel like some sort of dance that you learned and you know by heart. That's not only you. It's your own way of talking to the spirits. I may be able to talk to more of them, but you two are able to talk to your close spirits more deeply. You don't always have to use words to have a conversation. Sometimes you just feel it."

Nichelle and Clark were silent, staring at the table in deep thought. I got a little nervous. I had never had such an honest conversation about spirits with anyone before. In truth, nobody had ever really wanted to know. Having grown up around the spirits, it had never been strange to me, but I assumed for someone who was hearing this for the first time, it could be life-changing.

At that moment, Peter hurried to the table, his hood drawn around his serious face. There was a change though, something that could've been a mixture of impatience and excitement. He sat directly across from me and took a deep breath. He nodded.

My head snapped up. Our eyes met. There was an unmistakable gleam of pride in his gaze.

"You found something," I half-asked, half-guessed.

A small smile tugged on the corner of his mouth. "Yes."

"Peter," Clark said, eyes wide as his brain was probably working harder than it ever had, "did you know Toki talks to spirits? She can hear all sorts of things—like my guitar pick, and trash cans, and dogs, and..."

Peter waved him off, disinterested. "Yes, I know."

"You do?" Nichelle and Clark asked at the same time, flabbergasted.

He looked at them both and shrugged. "Yes. She talks to spirits. What's the big deal?"

For the first time in my life, I finally felt like I was accepted. I wanted to run across the table and hug Peter, but I'm sure the school had some pretty solid rules about PDA in the cafeteria. I settled for a grateful smile.

"Anyway," he continued, a little irritated that he had been interrupted, "I asked my mother if you could come to my house tonight for dinner. All of you. I can show you what I found."

Nichelle and Clark now were both staring at Peter. Suddenly my revelation about talking to the spirits of the world didn't seem half as crazy as Peter inviting us all over to his house for dinner, let alone the fact that he was speaking to us in the first place.

He hurried on. "It's Spring Festival. We have so many dumplings at home. Too many." He groaned slightly at the thought. "Mother is always asking if I have friends that want to come over. I figured we could meet tonight and solve many different problems."

"I'm in," I responded.

Clark gave a catty grin. "I'll be there. I'm so happy this day has finally come. I knew that you and I were destined to be friends from the moment we sat at the table together." He watched fondly as Peter flipped him off indifferently. "Aw, look. He's speechless."

Nichelle, it seemed, was having a harder time than Clark at wrapping her mind around everything. She stood and stared at us all, as if she were unsure of who we really were. She opened her mouth for a moment, then stopped. Shaking her head, she grabbed her backpack and quickly walked away.

Peter glanced at me. "What's wrong with her?"

"She didn't know that spirits talk. I think I just blew her mind today. She'll probably need a moment to herself," I said, wishfully thinking aloud. I hoped I hadn't just ruined a possible friendship. Despite her prickly attitude, Nichelle was rational, brave, and determined. I wanted to have her on my side certainly more than having her against me.

"Oh." Peter glanced at Clark. "I'm assuming you just learned about spirits today, too? You seem to be taking it well."

Clark grinned excitedly as he rubbed the guitar pick between his thumb and forefinger. "Yeah. I read comic books, remember? I've basically been training for this moment for forever. I'm not going to look a gift horse in the mouth. Especially if there's free dumplings involved."

"Okay," Peter said, looking pleased with himself. "I'll text everyone directions to my house. See you at 7:00."

"Do you need our phone numbers?" I asked Peter.

"No," Peter replied in a strange tone I didn't understand until later. "I already have them."

I WAS LATE, rushing across the yard to Peter's house from my own. With no time to change, I was still in my tacky work uniform with my hair piled unceremoniously in a messy bun on top of my head. I was surprised to see Nichelle waiting in front of Peter's house, dragging her foot in the snow. Her head was down; when she heard me, her eyes snapped up and stared at me uncertainly for a moment.

"Hi," I said, trying desperately to break the ice. "You decided to come."

She bit at her lip. "Yeah. I got a text from Peter. It's a little weird because I don't recall ever giving my number out—to anyone."

"I know," I sympathized. "I'm a little curious about that part too."

She looked at me for a moment, and I thought I saw her eyes soften. I stood there shivering. I was in too much of a hurry to put on my jacket, and although I was freezing, the fact that Nichelle was here made me feel better.

Finally she said, "Oh my God. Do you actually have to wear that shirt at work?"

I laughed. "Yeah. In case you're wondering, no, they don't pay me double for the humiliation."

Nichelle put her hand up to her mouth and chuckled. "It's awful, Toki."

"Trust me, I know. Once my dad gets an idea in his head, it's nearly impossible to talk him out of it."

We sat there giggling for a moment in the snow before the front door opened. Peter and Clark looked out curiously.

"So..." Clark began, "are you two just going to stand out there, or are Peter and I going to have to start our super-secret club by ourselves?"

Peter looked pained and gave me a silent look that begged me to come in. I could only imagine the courage it took him to invite Clark over to his home and entertain him single-handedly for fifteen minutes. I glanced at Nichelle.

"Are you okay? I mean, at lunch, you..."

She waved her hand, cutting me off. "Forget it. I mean, yeah, the fact that you can talk to these spirit... things... is pretty weird, but it's not any weirder than Clark, so you're good by me." She walked brusquely in the front door.

"How rude! I think you're just worried Peter found something better than you and is going to be released from detention first," Clark responded back.

We all introduced ourselves to Peter's mother and thanked her profusely for dinner. She seemed over the moon that Peter was bringing anybody home, and I guessed that it had probably never happened before. We loaded plates full of steaming dumplings and took them into Peter's room. I shut the door behind me and stared in wonder.

"Whoa. This is amazing," I breathed.

Suddenly, Peter's affinity for electronics made sense. His room was covered with all sorts of different gadgets. I counted no fewer than fourteen different types of tablets, laptops, desktops, and smartphones scattered in all parts of his room. Electronics crowded every open space, screens lighting up the room with a gentle blue glow. Shelves littered with wires, metal parts, computer chips, and batteries lined the room. At the very top of a bookcase sat an expensive-looking drone. I whistled when I saw it, glad that it was high out of reach from Clark's destructive hands.

"That's nice!" I said, pointing up to it.

I could feel Peter radiating with pride. "Yes. My grandfather bought that for me last Chinese New Year. I... haven't flown it yet." He was quiet for a moment, then he beckoned us over to his desktop computer, shoving empty Doritos bags and bottles of Mountain Dew to the floor.

Nichelle looked disgusted. "You need to clean!" she admonished, gingerly moving a dirty sock from a desk chair in the corner.

Clark and I stood over Peter as he logged into one of the most impressive-looking desktop computers I'd ever seen. The screen was almost as large as my television back home. He clicked a few buttons. Instantly, a log of text messages popped up.

"I was able to pull the last fifty or so texts that Liam sent," Peter said.

Clark's eyes grew wide as he scanned the computer screen. "Not bad, Pete, not bad! How did you pull this off?"

Peter scrolled down on the computer, shrugging nonchalantly. "Not a big problem. Just needed a new battery. The screen was trashed, so I had to download all of it onto the computer. It was password protected, but I logged into the school database. Was able to guess it in five tries."

"Logged?" Nichelle asked dubiously. "You mean 'hacked', right? Is that how you got our phone numbers, too?"

Ignoring the question, Peter continued. "Anyway, I found that the pass-code was recently changed. All of Liam's passwords used to be Sydney Wellington's birthday, but it seems like he changed his phone code the night of the 3rd. Once you see this last text exchange, you'll get why he changed it."

He moved from the chair and let me sit down in front of the screen. I took a deep breath and read them aloud.

Sydney: where'd u go?
Sydney: hello???
Sydney: plz talk 2 me
Sydney: it was mikes idea
Sydney: Im sorry we've been together so long I don't want 2 lose u
Liam: Sorry doesn't fix this. It doesn't fix "us." We're done. Tell Mike to screw off when I'm sure you'll see him next.
Sydney: Liam stop it can u plz pick up and talk 2 me???

Nichelle scratched at her head. "Yikes."

"Yeah," Clark nodded, "her grammar is atrocious."

I stared at the screen, thinking to myself. Mike, Sydney, Coach Rossi, Ashley, Liam—something happened that connected everyone together the fateful night of the wrestling meet. It had to be something huge. How did Liam go from star athlete, scholarship nearly locked in, beautiful girlfriend completely devoted and maybe a tad bit obsessed, to this?

Nichelle leaned forward with her head in her hands. "It's kinda sad. I mean, I didn't like Liam, but no one deserves this. It seems like in one night, he lost everything."

"Not lost," I mused aloud. "Look at these texts. He didn't lose his best friend and his girlfriend. He pushed them away. It's like he's making a choice."

"So what happened to make him make that choice? Those jerks have all been best buds since elementary school. It must have been something really bad to make them turn on each other like that," Nichelle responded.

"That's not all I found."

We all turned to look at Peter.

"You mean you hacked into a broken phone, found all these messages, AND found something else?" Clark asked. "Oh man, I think I'm out of the running for Best Buzzer."

Peter leaned over me and tapped the keyboard. A new window popped up. It was the black and white footage of a snowy parking lot at night in outstanding HD clarity.

Nichelle squinted at the screen. "You've got to be joking. I recognize that place. That's the parking lot behind the athletic lockers."

"You hacked into the school security system?" I asked, impressed.

Peter shrugged modestly. "Eh. They store all the footage on a cloud-base server. Someone at the district level isn't very creative when it comes to logins and passwords. They use the same password for every account."

Eyes wide, I clicked on the 'PLAY' button. "Remind me never to get on your bad side."

In the upper-left hand corner, the time clicked by steadily: 19:52, 19:53. Snow fell in front of the camera in large flakes, adding to the already thickening drifts piling up on the cars.

"I remember that night! There was a big snowstorm that missed everyone's radar. That was a hairy ride home in the Clark-mobile," Clark exclaimed, his eyes glued to screen.

I wanted to point out that every ride home in Clark's ridiculous van could be considered 'hairy', but my thoughts were interrupted. As the camera clicked to 19:58, a figure emerged from the side athletic door and stormed through the parking lot. With an agitated motion, the person swept snow off of a motorcycle, quickly threw a helmet on, and peeled out of the parking lot. My stomach was queasy. No one should drive that fast let alone on a night where the roads were surely icing over quickly.

Peter rubbed his chin. "That's Liam. He's the only one at school with a motorcycle. Keep watching. It gets more interesting."

20:05. Another figure in a heavy coat stepped out in the cold. The thick flakes of snow had gathered on the camera lens, making it harder to see than before. The figure ambled out, slipping slightly on the pavement. After a moment staring at the spot where Liam's motorcycle had just been, the figure moved toward the back of the parking lot and disappeared off-camera. A moment later, a dark colored truck drove to the exit of the parking lot. The vehicle seemed to have some troubles starting and stopping, seeming like it was stuttering whenever it accelerated. Must be the icy roads, I thought to myself. The truck left the parking lot and followed the motorcycle's disappearing tracks.

"Who's that?" I asked.

Silence filled the room. I looked at Nichelle and Clark. They shrugged.

"Not sure. Lots of people have trucks at school," Nichelle said.

"It's too far away to see a license plate," Clark added. "It's going to be impossible to figure out."

Peter spoke up. "Not impossible, just time-consuming. If I can check all the cameras around the gym that night, I might be able to compile a list of most of the people who were at the wrestling meet. I can then cross-reference that to a list of truck owners with the parking pass registration on the school data base."

Clark jumped up excitedly, grabbing at his hair. "That's right! Everyone who parks at the school has to buy that stupid parking pass and fill out the registration form. That will have everyone's vehicle description in one place." Peter nodded as Clark danced around the room. "Oh man, I take back every bad thing I ever said about you, Pete. You're a genius!"

"My only concern is that I don't know a lot of names. Trying to figure out who everyone is may be hard," Peter admitted sheepishly. "I... tend to keep to myself."

"I know most of the fools in the school. I'll come over and help tomorrow," Nichelle offered.

Peter looked grateful. "Thanks. I'll start what I can tonight."

"Great," I said, standing up. "We've got a plan at least. Text me when you find something."

Peter nodded. "Will do."

Nichelle frowned. "Should I ask how you got our numbers all by yourself, or was it through one of your 'hacking' adventures?" When Peter didn't answer, she rolled her eyes. "Hmph. Whatever happened to the old-fashioned way of just asking?"

It didn't matter to me. As Nichelle, Clark and I left the house and stood in Peter's snowy driveway, I felt a glimmer of hope.

"We're finally getting somewhere," I said aloud, excitedly.

"I admit it, Toki, you got way farther with this investigation than I thought possible. I'm sorry I doubted you." Nichelle shoved a woolen cap over her springy hair. "Liam was no friend of mine, but he didn't deserve to die. Hopefully Peter and I can come up with something for you tomorrow."

I smiled. "It's okay, Nichelle. If some random girl came into my town and starting breaking into lockers, I wouldn't trust her…" I lost my train of thought as I remembered something. Lockers.

Digging into my pocket, I pulled out the mint tin that Sydney had angrily discarded into the bottomless pit of her locker that morning.

Use as directed! The pills shouted at me from within.

I handed it to Clark. "This is what Mike Treverly's been up to," I told them both.

He opened it, and both he and Nichelle stared unbelieving at the seemingly anonymous pile of white pills. He let out a whistle.

"I heard rumors about a pill-mill going around school, but I never thought it'd be Mike!"

"Yeah," Nichelle agreed. "He's so stupid, I can't believe he hasn't gotten caught yet."

"Well, here's the part that's weird. Liam was suspended from the wrestling team the night of the state qualification meet because an anonymous tipster reported he had some of these pills in his locker. Mike's locker, we can assume, was clean, because he wasn't suspended and went on to win," I informed them.

Nichelle shrugged. "Mike was lucky, then. Maybe he moved his stash before that night. Liam was taking pain killers to get high and got caught. What's that got to do with anything?"

I crossed my arms, taking a deep breath. "I'm not so sure he was."

"What does that even mean?" she asked.

"Follow me on this. I found a random pill bottle in Liam's locker. Coach Rossi must have confiscated the one from the search, so I think this one was put in his locker after the search as insurance that when the school security team searched it, they would find even *more* evidence. Liam was allowed in his locker before he went home that night, so he must have seen it. I think he knew he was being set up. He ripped up the suspension letter because he was so mad and threw that and the pill bottle back into the locker and left on his motorcycle. He didn't even take his jacket! He was so upset he probably didn't even think about how dangerous it was to ride his motorcycle home in a snow storm."

Clark blinked at me. "You think that Mike set him up?"

I shrugged. "Think about it, Clark. With Liam suspended, Mike actually has a shot to get to the state championship. He'll get the scholarship then. Mike is dating Ashley at the time, who is the team wrestling manager. She has access to all of the athletic locker rooms during the meet, especially since Nichelle told me Rossi leaves his keys just lying around all the time."

She nodded. "True. That's how I got them. It was easy. He didn't even know they were gone. I had them for over two hours."

Clark furrowed his brow. "So you think Ashley planted the pills in Liam's locker both times because Mike charmed her into doing it."

Nichelle gagged. "Then she's an idiot, too."

"I think Liam thought the whole drug suspension was a mistake at first. However, Ashley and Mike weren't counting on the fact that Liam would go back to his athletic locker before leaving. He must have found the second pill bottle that wasn't there ten minutes ago and figured out what was going on."

Clark thought about that a moment as he scratched at his sandy hair. "That explains why Liam was angry at Mike. Doesn't really explain why he and Sydney broke up almost immediately afterward."

I nodded. "I know. That's why I've got to try to talk to Sydney tomorrow. I need to figure out what happened between the two of them."

"Too bad tomorrow is Saturday," Clark sighed. "It'd be easy to find her at school, but it's going to be impossible on the weekend."

"Batman could do it," Nichelle said nonchalantly.

We both turned to her.

"What did you say?" Clark asked, convinced he hadn't heard her correctly.

"You heard me. Batman would have no trouble tracking her down, even on a Saturday. Shame that you can't."

I grinned. Nichelle was an evil genius. Good thing she was in my corner.

A determined grim look crossed Clark's face. I could almost see a cape flying behind him in the wind as he stood up a little straighter.

"You're right," he said in a weird, gravelly voice which I assumed was what Batman sounded like. "Crime doesn't take a break. I'll find her tomorrow, Toki, if it's the last thing I do."

I shot a thankful look at Nichelle who brushed it off like it was no big deal. We all exchanged phone numbers the good old fashioned way. I said good night to them both and began my short walk across the lawn to my house.

Something was still puzzling me about the note that I had found in Liam's athletic locker. There was something strange about it, but for the life of me I couldn't figure it out. Walking inside my house, I sent a text to Peter.

Quick question while you're hacking. Sorry to interrupt. Was Liam ever at the detention table with you all?

I got an instant reply from Peter which was gratifying.

Peter: No.

I scratched at my head and furiously fired off another text.

Can you check Liam's record for any suspensions or office referrals?

Peter: Just did on a hunch. Nothing. Not even a tardy. He had a spotless record.

That was odd. How could Liam have been suspended from all school activities when he wasn't even on the administrator's radar?

I assumed something as serious as drug possession would be logged into the system right away for accountability and legal purposes. If there was nothing in the system, though, it was almost like nothing had ever happened.

There was still something in that letter that was nagging me. I had to go back and look at all the evidence again.

I went into my room and glanced at grandmother's clock. It still stubbornly read February 4th.

I shook my head. Why did Grandmother see the need to give me an old broken clock? I put my hand on top of it, predicting what it was going to say. What it did say next was a complete surprise.

Not broken. Important!

I stared at it for a moment. It wasn't broken? Maybe it was delusional. Some spirits liked to believe they were still useful and beautiful when they were beyond all hope of repair. Something sat with me uneasily as I thought about the date.

The wrong date had read February 5th when I received the clock. Now a day later, it was February 4th. That would make tomorrow February 3rd ... the day that Liam had died.

I suddenly had a horrible realization. The clock was right; it wasn't broken, and it certainly was important.

Rule one: the clock is both your enemy and your friend.

Sheriff Rankin had implied I had a time limit to solve this crime. What if the clock was showing my time limit? What if I had to solve the crime before Liam died, all according to Grandmother's clock?

That meant I had one day to put this all together.

Needless to say I didn't sleep very well that night.

Chapter Eleven: Grandmother Emi

Saturday, February 13th. 3:13 p.m.

MOM AND I SAT in Grandmother's room, each with own hopes that she would wake up and our own anxieties that she wouldn't.

We had come right at the beginning of afternoon visiting hours. My mother tried to chat cheerily to Grandmother about little things, but I could tell it was difficult for her. Part of me wondered what would happen if her mother ever woke up. If she could barely talk to her when she was unresponsive, how would she act when they actually had a real conversation?

Finally, Mom fell into a silence. We didn't even have the ticking of a clock to fill the room.

Speaking of ticking clocks, I couldn't help but think I was wasting my time here. I kept checking my phone against all the rules posted in the room, waiting for a text from anyone. Nothing. I needed a miracle if I was going to solve this killing in time.

At that moment, I got one, just not exactly the kind of miracle I was expecting.

There was a knock at the door that nearly sent my mother and I flying out of our seats. A familiar grizzled face popped in.

"Uh, excuse me. I'm sorry to interrupt."

I stopped myself from gasping audibly. Sheriff Rankin stepped in with his hat in his hands. Surely he was here to arrest me, I thought to myself. Maybe I shouldn't have called him old so many times. I got ready to stand up and present my hands. At least he couldn't add "resisting arrest" to the charges.

To my surprise, he completely ignored me and turned to my mom. "Mei Tooley? I'm Sheriff Rankin. I was wondering if I could have a word with you privately in the hall?"

Mom stood up, quizzically looking at the sheriff. "Yes, of course. Toki, I'll be right back."

As she stepped out in the hallway, Rankin lingered in the doorway for a moment. He winked at me and nodded over to the bed. He mouthed the words *Five minutes.*

I looked back at the bed. Grandmother Emi was sitting up and watching me with bright eyes and a serene smile.

"I bet you have questions," she said in a low, pleasant voice. She patted the bed beside her as I walked over numbly. "We don't have much time now, do we? If your mother sees me awake, you may never have time to finish the job you've started."

It took me a moment to find my voice. "Have you been faking?" I asked.

Grandmother Emi shrugged her thin shoulders. "Not as much as you may think. My mind, Toki… it's not what it used to be. My body seems to rebel against me every day. One day, I collapsed, and I woke up here. I was too weak to investigate what happened to Liam. That's why I choose you, Toki. You listen to the spirits; you have the courage. I know that you can save them."

A mixture of emotions swirled in my stomach, making me feel nauseous. Frustrated, I blurted out, "How? Liam's already dead. There's nothing I can do about it now."

"Oh, child, I know that the journal told you the rules. What is rule five?"

I thought about it for a moment. "Second chances only are given to all who accept them."

"Everyone deserves a second chance, and you are the one who can give it to them. If you find the answer, you can right the terrible wrong that has happened. It's the only way to bring peace back to Devil's Ford." She arched an eyebrow at me. "You've felt the Dark Spirit, haven't you?"

I nodded. I could still feel the icy touch of the spirit on my fingertips, through my hair, swirling around my feet. It was an unshakable feeling that was always there since the other night. There had been a spirit. It had touched me. It had hurt me.

"Imagine that feeling spreading across the town, my dear one. Everything that Dark Spirit touches feels the same pain you felt. Maybe not as intense, but it is a slow icy burn that permeates the soul of every spirit. The infection spreads as the Dark Spirit travels, contaminating everything in its reach. Devil's Ford—this tiny, innocent town—will not be able to bear the weight of such spirits for long. That is our job, my dear. We are the Protectors of this town."

"We are Protectors," I repeated, trying to understand everything my grandmother was saying. "We protect the town from… from the Dark Spirit? How?"

Grandmother gave me a meaningful smile. "Remember the rules. Let's review, shall we, and see how much you've learned by yourself?"

Rule one: the clock is both your enemy and your friend.

"The first rule tells me that I have a time limit. From what I can tell, the clock you gave me lets me know what my time limit is. I have until the actual time of the death to solve the crime," I said, fairly confident I had solved this riddle.

Grandmother nodded encouragingly at me.

Rule two: their future is not your future.

I had to think about that one. The clock goes backward to the day of the death. Why? If the clock's future was the past, then I suppose that our futures would be different. But why the word "their" instead of "its" or "the clock's"?

"Rule two makes my head hurt," I told Grandmother.

She laughed. "That's normal. I always have trouble remembering that one. It doesn't get any easier. Let's move to rule three."

Rule three: Write the name but be certain—there is no going back.

This had to do with the journal. I pulled it out from my pocket and flipped through the pages. There were names, dates, places, the strange embossed stamp on most of the entries. As I looked closer, however, I realized there was a large space just above each embossed symbol.

I frowned. "I write the name…of the killer?" I turned to Grandmother, raising an eyebrow. "If that's the case, why are there no names at the end by the stamp?"

Grandmother shrugged. "Second chances," was all she said.

Well that was infuriating. I huffed and continued on.

Rule four: Only those who approach the light will remember.

"Okay, well. The next rule is something with approaching a light." I stopped and thought for a moment. Light, dark. Surely they must be connected somehow. "Is that how the Dark Spirit is defeated? The Light defeats it?"

Grandmother smiled. "Something like that. You're getting closer."

She was displaying far more optimism than I was feeling. It seemed like the more that I talked to Grandmother, the more uncertain I became. When she saw the look on my face, she took my hand gently.

"You may not ever completely understand, Toki, but you will grow to accept this gift that's been given to us. Remember, you don't have to be alone. You must not be alone. Friends must walk beside you into bitter winds to make them easier to bear. Take their hands, but be ready. Once the light guides you, the race is on. Then we come to rule five."

I nodded without any clue of understanding. "The second chances one."

"Yes, and the most important," Grandmother added. "That is the true way we protect the town. Toki, I'm so proud of you. You have figured out so much on your own. Foster was unsure if you could do it, but now surely he will understand that you are our only hope."

"Foster?"

Grandmother Emi laughed quietly. "Oh, forgive me. He is so slow to trust, I should have realized it would take time. Foster is the name of my dearest friend, and soon to be one of your friends, I hope. He is the sheriff."

I snorted. "Sheriff Rankin, my friend? Yeah right. I wouldn't hold your breath."

"People will surprise you, Toki. They still surprise me to this day. I think you and Foster will be good friends sooner than you think."

I sighed for a moment. "It feels like my life has turned upside-down. Am I ever going to understand anything again?"

She smiled at me. "You know so much already. Trust yourself. Our time is nearly up. Remember the rules. They will guide you. Use your head but never forget your heart. It is the most important part of your spirit."

Nodding weakly, I squeezed her hand slightly. "I won't let you down."

Taking a deep, relaxed breath, Grandmother closed her eyes and smiled. "I believe that, my child. Now it's time for you to believe it, too."

As I sunk down into the front seat of the car, my head spun with a million thoughts. First and foremost was that I was running out of time. Knowing that the clock in my bedroom was right, I had until a little past eight to stop the dark spirit and bring light back to Devil's Ford. I felt so far from the answer. Without any news from Peter, Clark, or Nichelle, I was stuck.

"You look down," my mom observed as she started the car.

"Something wrong?"

I shook my head. Even if I wanted to tell my mom what was going on, I wasn't sure I even knew enough to explain it coherently.

"It's nothing," I said. "Um… what did that policeman want?"

"Oh, nothing too important. He wanted to meet me. He's known Grandmother for awhile, but since it's been so long since I've been back here, we've never met."

We sat in silence for a moment. I bit my lip, wondering if I should ask the question that was orbiting around my mind for the past week. I took a chance.

"Mom, why did you leave this place? Why have we never visited Grandmother until now?"

She paused as she stared out the foggy window into the bleak winter air. I could see the wheels turning in her head, wondering how much she should tell me. I looked out the window at the road. A thin coat of ice frosted the pavement.

"This place," Mom began tentatively, "it's hard to explain to people who don't live here. There is a… heaviness here. Maybe you can feel it in some of the spirits that you've talked to?"

I tried to act surprised, but she smiled at me.

"Oh, I know you better than you think. You may have fooled your father, but the morning I saw the rock in the backyard that had the red flower on it, I knew."

She was good. I nodded. "Yeah. The spirits here are different from the ones back home. Heavy is a good word for it."

"I used to speak to the spirits, too. Just like you." My mother smiled, allowing herself to remember. "I had a good childhood. There was nothing but fond memories. My mother and my father, the spirits, it was all seemingly perfect. Then one day, after my fifteenth birthday, everything changed. It was sudden. One day everything was normal, and the next day my mother began hovering over me like a hawk. I wasn't allowed out of her sight; not away to volleyball games in different towns, or parties, or sleep-overs with friends. It's not that she didn't love me any less. She seemed to love me too much. She wanted to know my every movement, interrogated me about what was happening at school, who I was hanging out with, who I interacted with. I wasn't my own person anymore. My future was tied into her need for me."

She stopped at a red light and took a breath. I stared at her, stunned. This was the most I had ever heard her say about Grandmother in one setting. Not only that, but she had also mentioned her father. It was a topic I had never heard her speak of before.

"I needed space. My own friends, my own life that was separate from hers. I wanted something she couldn't possibly pry into anymore. So I moved away, far away, the minute that I graduated from high school. I never looked back."

It took me a moment to find my breath. "What about your dad?"

My mother looked like she had been punched in the stomach. Her hands tightened around the steering wheel.

"My father was murdered a year after I left for college. They never found his killer. That's why it has been difficult, maybe impossible, to come back here to visit. I had to leave, you see, but your Grandmother refused to go with me. We talked about it, argued about it for ages and ages. Finally, I gave up. I didn't understand how she could still be so committed to a place where my father had drawn his last breath, especially knowing his killer was out there somewhere."

I was quiet. For a town that had bragged about its safety record, the fact that my own grandfather had been murdered was a bitter pill to swallow.

"Grandmother stayed for his spirit?" I half-guessed.

Mom nodded. "Yes. Looking back on it, knowing what I know about our family and our... abilities... I'm sure that's what it was. He was still here, somehow. She didn't want to leave him. At that point, I stopped hearing the spirits. Maybe I just stopped listening to them, I don't know. When my father died I just didn't seem to care what anyone had to say anymore. It took meeting your father to wake me up again and see the light. After blocking out the spirits for so long, though… well, I forgot how to hear them. Honestly, not hearing them anymore has made it bearable to move back here."

That thought was terrifying to me. I couldn't imagine what it would be like not to hear the giggle of a jump rope, the sad sigh of a falling leaf, or the stately greetings of an ancient piece of driftwood. To lose that would be like losing part of myself.

My mother tried to smile light-heartedly at me. "That's why I've tried to give you some freedom your whole life. My mother never seemed to trust me after that strange day even though I had done nothing wrong. I made a promise to myself that once I had my own children, I would honor their independence. I've tried to remember this every day with you and Ken. I trust you. You know if there's ever anything you need…"

"I can come to you," I finished. "I know mom. Trust me, the whole independence thing is appreciated."

The fact that mother and Grandmother Emi were always at such odds seemed to make more sense now, though I knew I was only hearing half the story. It seemed so strange and so awful. To feel trapped in a place with a person who couldn't let you out of their sight, ever? I couldn't imagine how I would respond, though I'm sure moving far away from Devil's Ford would certainly seem like the only solution.

At that moment, my phone buzzed. I looked and saw a text from Clark.

Clark: Found Sydney. Guess who she's with? If you hurry to the Elm Street Diner, you can get a two-for-one special. Wink wink.

Wink wink? Who texted that instead of just using a winking emoji? I didn't have time to probe the mystery of Clark's brain. I understood immediately who he had seen.

"Hey mom, speaking of independence and doing my own thing, do you think you can drop me off somewhere? I'm going to meet Clark and..."

The minute I said it, I instantly regretted it. I saw the corner of my mom's mouth tugging into a smile.

"No," I said firmly. "No, no, no. Not like that. Clark's a friend. Kinda. Except he's really annoying sometimes."

My mom nodded understandingly. "Mmm. I see. Like a bad habit you can't get rid of, huh? Believe it or not, I used to think your father was the same way..."

She then launched into her story about how she and Dad met at the dentist's office which I had only heard about 75 times before. I zoned out and stared through the window. Something my mom said tickled at the back of my brain. *Like a bad habit.* I turned the phrase over and over in my mind, wondering why it was bothering me so much. For the life of me, I couldn't place it. Maybe it was just the fact that Mom's bad habit was Dad, who she eventually ended up marrying. Applying that same logic to Clark was simply unacceptable.

Chapter Twelve: Suspicions

IN THE SPIRIT WORLD there are some places that are just humming with gossip. You can feel it right when you walk in the front door. It's like a million ears just waiting to hear what you're going to say, and a million mouths just waiting to repeat it all back to anyone willing to listen.

I try to stay away from these places. It's usually a sensory overload in there. So many spirits are always listening and trying to get your attention that it's not really a place you can relax for long. Usually these places are also popular. People will say the place has a certain "buzz" or "atmosphere." That would be the spirits' doing. Places like that have a lot of people, which until recently was not exactly the kind of place you would find me at.

Elm Street Diner was one of those places. I could hear it humming from the car as soon as I opened the door. There was a lot of buzz going on in that little diner. I took a deep breath and waved goodbye to my mother.

A charming bell above the door announced my arrival. A sign in the corner told me to seat myself. I noticed Clark sitting at a counter, swirling a straw around a chocolate milkshake with a bright red maraschino cherry on top. He locked eyes with me, but instead of saying anything, tilted his head toward a booth near the back.

They were still both there. Sydney and Mike sat opposite each other at a booth, heads down low as they talked in furious whispers back and forth. There was something very wrong with this scene, I thought to myself. Liam had died, cold and alone, on the side of the road ten days ago. He was a young, handsome, and talented kid with his whole life ahead of him. Now he was stuck forever at 17 in a grave. Seeing these two—supposedly the two closest people in his life—chatting it up together like some sort of conspiracy was unnerving to me.

Luckily the two were too busy talking to each other. They didn't notice me. I placed my hand on the booth next to them and listened.

Help me, I pleaded, *what have they been talking about?*

Maybe I had been too harsh in my opinion of diners. This place actually was helpful. The booth was only too obliged to answer.

Lies.

Lies. A conspiracy. These two must have been in it together, but how? Mike Treverly certainly benefitted from getting Liam thrown off the wrestling team, but why would Sydney get involved? Would she really want him to lose his scholarship, lose his spot at...

I stopped in my tracks, remembering what my mother had just said.

I wasn't my own person anymore. My future was tied into her need for me.

A chill ran through my body like the Dark Spirit itself had just grabbed my hand. I suddenly had a clear vision of why Sydney was involved in all of this and why she needed to lie. The thought of it made me sick to my stomach.

There was only one way to confirm the answers to the questions I had. I needed to pretend like I knew everything. That way if I was way off-track, it'd be obvious. This was going to be a solo endeavor.

Throwing on an air of devil-may-care confidence, I bravely strolled up to the booth and slid in next to Mike.

"Hey guys," I said, grabbing a menu and pretending to browse the daily specials.

They both stared at me as if I had three heads.

"Um, excuse me, this is a private conversation," Sydney informed me with the largest amount of disgust that she could muster. "Can you leave?"

I counted to ten then slowly placed the menu down. "Don't worry. I won't be here for long." I turned to Mike and stuck out my hand. He ignored me with every blood cell in his body. "The name's Toki Tooley. I'm new here in town. See, I'm just a little nosy, and there's this rumor going around school. I have to ask you two about it because I'd hate to spread gossip that wasn't true."

Mike's posture stiffened as he looked at me. "Rumor?"

Sydney stared at me as though she wanted to drag me out of the booth by my hair.

I grabbed a tortilla chip from the basket in the middle of the table, dipped it into some salsa, and chewed it up. "So tell me, when did you two decide you were going to plant the pills in Liam's locker? I mean I know how you did it. Mike, you used your muscle head charm to get Ashley to do it for you, and then you dumped her like a garbage bag right after. That part makes complete sense to me even if it does make you a bit of a pig. Here's the thing I can't figure out—did you do it before or after the wrestling meet had started?"

Sydney and Mike stared at me, mouths open.

I continued, enjoying myself too much to stop. Plus, the chips and salsa were way better than I had anticipated. "Here's how I think it happened, but please stop me if I'm wrong. Mike, I heard you're pretty good at wrestling, but I think Liam was always just a little better than you. Maybe a lot better. You knew this, Coach Rossi definitely would've known this, so it shouldn't have been any big surprise about who was going to win that spot at State and the scholarship at the end of the night. Imagine, though, what would happen if Liam was just out of the way for a little bit? If you could get him disqualified from that last meet, then maybe you'd get the spot for state. I think it was an awful, toady thing to do to your best friend, but I see why you got Ashley to plant those drugs in his locker. There was no other way you could guarantee your win."

Mike shook his thick head, stuttering. "No. You've got it wrong. No one snitched on Liam. They did a random search of all the lockers right before the meet. It was just bad timing on his part, yeah?"

I nodded sympathetically. "That was the genius part of your plan, Mike. You blackmailed Rossi into conducting that random search so that Liam couldn't even step foot in the match. The interesting part to me is that this 'random search' was never reported to the administration. There's no record of the random search, or the drugs, or Liam's suspension. The admin didn't know, Liam's parents didn't know, and Liam certainly didn't know. How did you get Rossi to do your bidding? I'll bet all the money in my pocket that somehow you caught Coach Rossi and his drinking problem red-handed. You probably had enough evidence to not only make him lose his job but also lose his license or go to jail. Did you find the vodka bottles in the trash can?"

Mike's shocked face was all the answer I needed.

"Oh, don't be so surprised. I've been at that school for five days, and I can tell Rossi's hitting the bottle. It's all in the stumble and the smell." I glanced at Mike appraisingly. "You must have found something pretty bad for Coach Rossi to throw his best athlete under the bus."

I reached into my pocket, pulling out the torn-up letter that Nichelle and I had found in Liam's locker. Last night I had gone over it, line by line, looking for any clues I could find. The biggest clue had been right in front of my face. It had been what *wasn't* on the letter that had bothered me so much, and I finally realized it.

"See, this letter that Liam had torn-up was pretty important. It's signed by Coach Rossi. Do you see anything that's missing?"

The pair stared at me blankly.

"Don't feel bad. I didn't see it at first, either. I may be new to Chamberlain, but I know that all schools have a letterhead that they use on all letters sent out to parents. That way it's easy to tell if some kid is sending a phony letter home or if it's legit." I pointed to the top corner of the torn-up letter. "There's no letterhead here. This is an unofficial letter from Coach Rossi's computer that he typed up himself. Not only is it missing that official letterhead, but it is also missing signatures from any admin and from the head of security. The letter states that admin and security knew about the random drug search, but the lack of signatures proves that they didn't. It was all kept in-house and very hush-hush."

Mike visibly gulped. "What's that got to do with me?"

I ate another tortilla chip casually. "The date, February 3rd, shows that Liam wouldn't even get this letter until the day of the state qualification meet. He probably got it as soon as the meet started so that there'd be no time to protest. To Liam, it immediately barred him from competing, and the only thing he could do was go home. I'm guessing the plan was once the match was over and you've weaseled your way into state, Rossi would bring up the drug issues with the admin. They would conduct an investigation at that point. If Liam's found innocent, then it would be weeks later and far too late for him to compete at State, right?"

Thump. Sydney must have kicked a stunned Mike under the table. He immediately sprung to life, face burning into a bright red as he tugged the front of his ball cap down. I could smell sweat pouring through his shirt.

He tried to play it cool. "Whatever. I don't know what you're talking about. I made state fair and square. I even might have an athletic scholarship lined up for college."

Folding my hands together gravely, I nodded. "Yes. A scholarship that should have gone to Liam. He would have gotten it except being suspended from the wrestling team and missing state disqualified him. Now he would have a criminal record. College would probably be the last thing on this plate. There go all of his dreams and his future," I stopped for a moment, turning my gaze to Sydney, "being tied into your need for him."

Sydney began chewing at one of her fingernails. "Why are you looking at me? You've got a problem?"

I sighed. "I do have problems. Many, actually. Thanks for asking. For one, I don't know a lot of students at Chamberlain High School. Now, no offense Mike, but I've heard that you're not clever enough to plan this all by yourself. The question is who put this whole scheme into your brain?"

Flipping her gorgeous long hair out of her face, she turned away from me, rolling her eyes so dramatically she may have been staring at a spot on the ceiling. "Obviously you don't know anything about Liam and me. I loved him and he loved me. Why would I ever want to hurt him?"

My eyes flashed at her for a moment. Good question, I thought to myself.

"Of course you didn't want to hurt him," I responded coolly. "I think you wanted to keep him."

Sydney cocked her head at me. "What is that supposed to mean?"

"I'm thinking that Liam's plans for the future—going to a big college on a scholarship—somehow didn't include you. Did you know your homework assignments and tests are literally screaming for you to study harder? Now this is just a guess, but I'm assuming you applied to the same college as Liam, but you weren't accepted due to your GPA."

Sydney stood up angrily, her red hair flying in her face as she leaned toward me and whispered fiercely. "You think you're so smart, you stupid little loser? You think I'm the one who killed him? Well, news break, I don't even own a car. You come in here acting like you know Liam—well, you didn't. I did. He loved me. He told me that every day up until the day he died. It was one of the last things he said to me."

I shook my head, crossing my arms and leaning back into the booth. "That's not true. He actually texted that he never wanted to see you or Mike ever again."

Sydney and Mike had now turned a deathly shade of white. Sydney backed away slightly from the table, her fingers trembling.

"How could you possibly...?"

Strange, I thought to myself. You would think the revelation that I'd been chatting to her tests and homework assignments would have shocked her more than the fact that I knew about her last texts with Liam. I wondered vaguely why that was. I stood up, satisfied that I had confirmed most of my theories.

"I don't think what happened to Liam was a random hit-and-run. I think one of you, or maybe even both of you, killed him to cover up what you did. I will find out who it is and make sure this never happens again."

Mike made a desperate lunge, grabbing my arm violently with his meaty hands as he pulled me back into the booth. I winced as he squeezed hard, my body twisted at an awkward angle.

"What if we decide we don't let you, huh? You're just some new kid. You think anybody's going to really care if we decide to shut you up?"

"Let go of her, now."

A calm but dangerous sounding voice I had never before heard boomed from behind me.

When I looked back, I was shocked to see Clark standing nearby, shirt freshly stained with a drop of chocolate milkshake. He had an angry, serious face that I never could have placed on him before. He looked threatening enough to take on Nichelle. Mike's vice-like grip faltered when he saw Clark. It gave me enough time to break free from his grasp and make my escape from the booth.

"Toki's my friend," Clark said to the two of them, his voice low. It caused all three of us to shiver. "If you ever touch her again, I'm going to make sure you pay."

We left the restaurant in a hurry. I cradled my wrist and inspected it. There was definitely going to be a nasty-looking bruise there in the morning. As we walked across the parking lot to Clark's eagle van, I turned to him, heart bursting with gratitude.

"Thank you. That could've gotten very complicated if you didn't step in."

Clark shrugged nonchalantly. "I'm not going to stand by and watch my friends get threatened. That makes me angry. Did I seem angry? Sometimes my voice gets all gravelly and low, like Batman, and that's got to be super intimidating. Was I super intimidating?"

"Um, yeah Clark. You sounded exactly like... Batman."

Looking even more pleased with himself, Clark opened the front passenger door for me after a small struggle to unjam it. "Okay, let's stop talking about how cool I sounded for a minute and focus on you! I mean, you were amazing in there, Toki. You sounded exactly like a real detective. How did you manage to put that all together?"

Trying to hide a modest smile, I pulled Coach Rossi's letter to Liam from my pocket. "I didn't sleep very well last night. I spent most of the time looking at everything we had found. There was something off with that letter. Once I found out it was missing the letterhead, there was only really one reason why Coach Rossi would personally suspend his best athlete. He must have been blackmailed into doing it. Nichelle and I heard a phone conversation he was having. I think he was talking to Mike, saying that 'he wanted out' and 'you got what you wanted.' All of the pieces from that point just fell into place."

Clark whistled. "That's crazy, Toki. Remind me never to commit a crime with you in the neighborhood."

"We know what happened to Liam right up until the wrestling meet," I said, buckling my seatbelt and offering silent condolences to the van at the same time. "What we don't know, though, is what happened to him after he left."

My phone buzzed, as did Clark's. I looked down at the group text as Clark began typing a response immediately.

Peter: Come ASAP.

Clark: How about a please every now and then?

I sighed. "Why do you insist on antagonizing, Clark?"

Clark looked at his phone in amusement. "Watch this! 3... 2... 1... there! Awwww, a cute little emoji flipping me off! He's so predictable."

I shook my head, trying to keep my mind focused on Liam. I had to make an important decision between two names, and time was running out.

Chapter Thirteen: The Blue Truck

WITH THE THREE OF US sitting on Peter's bed, Peter said, "This is Mike Treverly's truck."

We all stared at him. Could it really be that easy?

"You sure?" I asked.

"Yes. 34 students own trucks, according to the parking pass vehicle registration list," Peter began. "Matching the surveillance video of the gym and entryways with all of the registered truck owners at Chamberlain, Nichelle and I came up with three possible suspects."

Nichelle pulled out her notebook and tapped the page. "Mr. Rossi, Mike Treverly, and Bailey Patterson were the only ones in attendance at that wrestling meet that own trucks."

Peter nodded his assent. "It can't be Rossi's truck because his is white. The truck in the video is a dark color. Bailey's had a dead battery that had to be jump-started after the meet. That, right there, has to be Mike's blue truck."

I nodded. "Wow, you two worked well together! Congratulations!" I turned to Nichelle but was surprised to see her face. She looked disappointed.

"What's wrong?" Clark asked her.

She mumbled, "Nothing. Just was hoping for it to be Rossi. Maybe it was a mistake. Maybe he had been drinking and driving and accidentally hit Liam in that snowstorm and didn't realize it. But for it to be Mike... I don't know. He and Liam were so close. It just seems really, really wrong that your best friend could knowingly kill you."

Peter nodded. "Yeah, but that's the evidence for you. It's pretty cut and dried."

Clark agreed. "Case closed, then. What happens now? Do we tell the Sheriff?"

I couldn't take my eyes off of the computer screen as Peter's loop of security footage rolled over and over. Nichelle was right. Something was nagging at the back of my brain.

"But why?" I asked aloud, seeming to startle everyone in the room.

"Why what?" Clark asked.

"Why kill him? It doesn't make sense. Liam was leaving the wrestling meet. He had already accepted that he couldn't compete, and it didn't seem like he raised a fuss as he left. He didn't text Mike anything, just Sydney telling them to stay away. Why would Mike need to kill him after that? He had everything he wanted."

Nichelle shrugged. "Treverly has a brain the size of a walnut, Toki. Nothing that kid does ever makes sense to me."

I had to look at my evidence again. I pulled out my journal from my pocket. Immediately, the familiar white light began winding around my wrists, urgently, and the book flew open to the last page as the rules were recited again.

Please sign your name with an acceptance or denial on the last page once you are ready to become a true Protector.

The journal trembled with energy, the light becoming brighter and brighter. Something was telling me my time was almost up.

The others in the room had jumped back and were staring at the light pouring from the journal into my hands. They could obviously see the spirit. I remembered the Sheriff had told me the closer you got to solving a mystery, the more obvious the spirit of the journal became. I was close.

"Whoa! What is that?" Clark asked, pointing.

Nichelle shook her head. "This is way weird, Toki. What's going on?"

Peter's eyes were wide, but he looked curious. He glanced at me with a questioning look.

"Spirits," he said, quietly.

I nodded. Keeping any more secrets at this moment seemed pretty pointless.

"My Grandmother used to solve crimes around here. When murders happen, this Dark Spirit comes around and threatens to swallow up the town with night and cold. Not just physical cold. It seems to grab hold of everyone's heart and all the spirits. It won't let them heal; it cripples the very soul of the town. If I can solve the murder, somehow the Dark Spirit goes away, and Devil's Ford heals."

"That seems a little vague on details," Nichelle pointed out. "How do you know it works?"

I shrugged. "I don't know how it works. Trust me, it does. The Sheriff knows that it does, my Grandmother knows. I don't know what's going to happen, but I know things will get better if I get this right." I looked at Peter, imploringly. "You believe me, don't you?"

Peter hesitated as he watched the white light winding around my wrists in a frenzy. He nodded slowly. "I do. My Grandfather always said this place was special. He said the spirits were stronger here. This must have been why he lived here."

"Soooooo..." Clark asked nonchalantly, motioning to the light, "what's going on there?"

Please sign your name with an acceptance or denial on the last page once you are ready to become a true Protector, the journal repeated patiently.

I grabbed a pen. "I think I have to sign my name. Then I'll take over my Grandmother's spot as Protector."

"Are you sure you want to do that?" Nichelle asked, incredulous. She was eyeing the journal on my lap as she backed away. "Maybe you've had chummy relationships with spirits all your life, but from what I know, spirits are evil and haunt things. You know, that white light looks like it's trying to tie you to that journal. Maybe that'll be forever? You want to be this... Protector thing forever?"

I glanced at Peter. He offered me a small smile.

"It's what I have to do," I said, hastily scribbling my name on the back page. "If I don't, this town will never be the same."

The ink on the last page shone brightly in white. At the same moment, the frenzied white light wrapping around my hands seem to fade into my skin, disappearing from view. When I looked down, I noticed the faintest trace of a white line around my wrists. I took a deep breath, having an uneasy feeling that I had pushed aside Nichelle's warnings too quickly. This did seem like a 'forever' thing. The journal immediately stopped repeating the command to me and sat silently on my lap.

Clark breathed a sigh of relief. "Nice job, Toki. At least that's one less spooky thing going on right now."

"Okay," I ventured shakily as I flipped the pages back to Liam's case. "My Grandmother told me to stop the Dark Spirit, I have to write the name of the guilty person and then follow the light."

Peter shrugged. "Easy, then. Write Mike Treverly's name. Everything points to him."

"Wait," Nichelle interjected, her sharp eyebrows raised. "What if you write the wrong name? You might not get a second chance, Toki."

You screw this up, just know—there are no second chances for anyone. That's what Sheriff Rankin had told me. Nichelle was right. If I wrote down the wrong guilty name, there may be no way to change my guess.

I thought about those few pages in the journal with the red mark. Were those the ones that Grandmother Emi had gotten wrong? If so, those names never had a second chance. No wonder Sheriff Rankin was so worried about me messing up. If I got it wrong, then the Dark Spirit would stay and feed off of the grieving.

"I don't know what to write," I admitted.

Everyone in the room was silent for a moment as we tried to think of what to do. Nichelle plopped down on the bed next to Clark and stuck her head in her hands. "If only we could..." She looked up, sniffing, then wrinkled her nose. "Clark! You stink!"

I rolled my eyes. "Nichelle, is this really the time..."

"She's right," Peter agreed, covering his mouth and nose with his shirt. "You smell like a giant armpit, Clark."

Despite all the frantic thoughts and worries running through my mind, I had to agree. Clark's scent was ballooning around the room like a toxic cloud.

"I'm sorry!" Clark exclaimed. "I'm a stress sweater! It's a medical problem where I sweat when I'm..."

"Stressed?" I guessed.

"Yeah! Wow, you're smart Toki! It's like you can read my mind!" He waited for me to be as impressed as he was. When he realized that was never going to happen, he awkwardly continued. "Ahem. Anyway, yeah, my mom calls it 'my condition' when my grandma's over so that we don't offend her, but it's not like a disease or anything. It's just a nervous habit or something."

As Peter rushed to open his window in the middle of a subzero February evening, I twirled the pen in my hand.

"Nervous habit," I murmured to myself. I thought back to my mom. Something reminded me of the phrase she had said that had jarred me earlier today.

Like a bad habit you can't get rid of, huh?

135

Bad habits. Noxious stress sweat was a pretty bad habit to have if you could take your pick. So was smoking. And laughing way too loud at inappropriate times. And...

I gasped. How could I have been so clueless?

"The fingernail polish," I breathed. "It said, 'wrong'. That's it!"

Nichelle, Peter, and Clark turned to me.

"What did you say?" Nichelle asked.

"The blue fingernail polish. When I was digging through Sydney's locker, she had all this trash at the bottom. There were these used bottles of blue fingernail polish. I think they even tried to warn me. They said, 'Wrong', like they were used for the wrong purpose!"

Peter blinked. "Still not connecting the dots, Toki."

"Don't you see?!" I exclaimed, pointing at the reeking Clark. "Bad habits. Nervous habits. Sydney has a nervous habit. She chews her fingernails when she's nervous. I can't believe I didn't notice it before; she does it all the time!"

Clark looked offended. "So what? Everyone who has a bad habit is a murderer? That's so judgmental, Toki."

"Think about it. Someone who chews their nails all the time would not also paint them."

Nichelle agreed, making a face. "No, that'd be nasty."

"Okay, we've established that she doesn't paint her nails. Why does she have empty fingernail polish in her locker?" Peter asked.

"Mike's truck," I revealed triumphantly. "Mike wasn't driving his truck when it left the parking lot. Sydney was. She doesn't have her own car, right? She gets this text from Liam breaking up with her. She's desperate to talk to him. She must have taken Mike's truck, whether he knew it or not, and chased Liam down. When she hit him, there might have been some light scratching or damage to the front of the truck. She must have gone to the store, bought the nail polish, fixed up the damaged part of the paint, and returned the truck before anyone knew she was gone and before the meet ended. I bet if we could look at Mike's truck now, we would be able to tell where she doctored it up. She must have done a good enough job to get by."

Clark's eyes lit up. "Right! That must be why we found the cellphone out in the bushes! Peter, you said that Liam changed his passcode on his phone the day he was killed, right? What if she knew there were incriminating texts on his phone that showed he had broken up with her just moments before?"

"So, she tries to get into his phone after she kills him and erase the break-up texts? Oh, that's cold!" Nichelle said, disgusted.

That's why Sydney was so upset when I had mentioned the texts between her and Liam at the diner. She knew at that point someone had found the phone that she had tried to hide. My eyes grew wide at the thought of it all coming together.

"The problem is, she can't get into his phone to get rid of the messages on his end," I continued. "She doesn't know the new passcode. Maybe out of frustration or fear, she takes the battery out of the cellphone, smashes the screen, and chucks it into the bushes hoping that it will never be found. At least it can give her some time to cover up her crime to look like a random hit-and-run."

Peter nodded his head. "It... makes sense."

Clicking the pen, I scribbled the name "Sydney Wellington" down, hoping that spelling didn't count against me. Everyone held their breaths as I finished the last letter and waited, my heart climbing into my throat.

Nothing happened.

Clark let out a breath. "Did it work?"

I frowned. "I don't think so... not yet. Grandmother mentioned something about following the light. I don't see a light anywhere!"

Nichelle bit her lip, worried. "Maybe we had it all wrong."

Peter looked toward his open window, blinking in surprise. "Um,

Toki, look at your house!"

I followed his gaze out the window. The sun had already set, and the cold night was completely dark, the moon and stars covered by thick snow clouds. Oddly though, a piercing white light broke the darkness from my room, shining so brightly that it made my blackout curtains look like cheesecloth. I blinked, surprised. Why did it seem as if my room was dripping in the highest-powered fluorescent light that man had ever invented? Just looking at it from Peter's room made my retinas hurt.

The journal buzzed slightly, warming under my hands. *Rule one: the clock is both your enemy and your friend.*

"The clock!" I gasped. "I think the light's coming from my Grandmother's clock. Follow me!"

I burst out of Peter's house, ignoring Nichelle's pointed questions about what a clock had to do with anything. I sprinted across the snowy yard and charged into my own house, closely followed by my friends.

Mom and Dad looked alarmed as I skidded through the front hallway.

"Hi Mom, Dad... this is Peter, Nichelle, Clark. Made some friends, aren't you proud of me?" I gasped as I bolted toward my room. "We've got some urgent Buzzer business, can't be disturbed, thanks, love you!"

Peter, Nichelle, and Clark quickly said hello then followed me to my room which was bathed in the bright white light I had seen from Peter's. I shut the door behind me loudly and prayed my parents remembered their whole 'respecting my space' vow.

"Wow, this is insane!" Clark said, marveling at the light. He had obviously not been taught never to look directly at the sun. "Your clock is the best night-light ever. Look at it! It could power a small village."

He was right. The light was coming from the clock.

Important, it had told me. Many times.

Now I understood why Grandmother wanted me to have the clock.

This was the way to defeat the Dark Spirit, though I wasn't exactly sure what was going to happen.

"We have to go into the light," I told the others.

"Are you sure that's a good idea?" Clark gulped, nervously. "Isn't that what you supposed to do when you die?"

"Do you see any other option?" Nichelle asked, shielding her eyes. "This thing is like a supernova. It's going to start attracting a lot of attention soon, and I don't exactly feel like explaining to the cops that this all started after we hacked into school security systems to try to solve a murder."

"What happens after we walk into the light?" Peter asked me.

"No idea," I admitted. "Grandmother said that the 'race' would be on, and that I could change everything with second chances. I guess we'll have to see. Um. I think we need to hold hands."

Nichelle rolled her eyes. "Oh, this just keeps getting better and better."

"Aww, Toki, any excuse to hold your hand is good enough for me," Clark cooed as he inconspicuously smelled himself. Seeming satisfied, he took my hand and Nichelle's. She gingerly took Peter's.

"Here goes nothing," I gulped, taking a deep breath as we all stepped toward the white light.

For a moment, I could see nothing. My sense of sight was completely overruled. I felt a chill that ran across my entire body as though I had been encased with ice. I could no longer feel Clark's hand in mine. As I raised my hand up to shield my eyes from the harsh glare, I could see a dark figure just before me.

It raised out its hand to me, gently.

I stopped in my tracks. It had to be the Dark Spirit. However, this time, I could tell it wasn't just the Dark Spirit. I knew exactly who it was.

"I'm coming to help you," I promised as I reached for its hand.

Chapter Fourteen: Liam

I OPENED MY EYES. For a moment, I was sure it had been a dream. I was crouched in the snow outside, and it was freezing. I shivered for a moment then looked beside me.

There was my backyard rock, freshly swept of snow. A single red carnation lay on top of it. I placed my hand on top of the rock and listened.

New? It asked brightly.

I gasped and pulled out my phone. February 3rd, 8:05 p.m. Somehow stepping into that light has sent me back to the night of Liam's murder.

Frantically, I checked my pockets for Grandmother's journal. It hadn't made the journey with me. I nearly face-palmed myself. Of course. If I had traveled back in time, I didn't have the journal yet. Grandmother Emi still had it with her. However, I very clearly remembered writing Sydney's name just before we all walked toward the light. If that was the case, and I was right about who killed Liam, then that meant...

Rule five: Second chances only are given to all who accept them.

Second chances. Of course! That's what Grandmother Emi, Sheriff

Rankin, and the journal had meant. Now, according to Grandmother, the "race was on." I jumped up from where I was sitting. It was now 8:05. That meant that Liam was still alive out there, but for how much longer?

I looked through my phone, scrolling through the contacts for Nichelle, Clark, or Peter's number. They weren't there. I groaned as the realization hit me. According to the laws of the universe, I technically hadn't met the three of them yet. They had come through the white light with me too, hadn't they? That meant that they were somewhere out there and hopefully had remembered everything I had.

I ran across my backyard toward Peter's house. My heart soared when I saw him fly out of his back door to meet me in his pajama pants, his hair a disheveled mess.

"You remember?" I asked as I met him at the fence dividing our backyards.

"Everything," he confirmed, suddenly seeming to realize he was in his pajamas. He reddened slightly. "Nichelle and Liam's phone numbers…"

"Yeah, I know. Listen, we don't have much time. Liam was found at 8:33, but I don't know when exactly he died. What's the fastest way to get to Delta Road?"

Peter jerked his thumb to the woods behind our houses. "Go in the woods. It's a straight shot to Delta Road, even faster than trying to drive there. You will have to go through the woods though, and it's completely dark outside. There's a chance you might get lost."

I nodded, shoving my hat back on my head. "Okay. Hopefully I can find Liam before it's too late."

Peter seemed to be thinking. He put up his finger for me to wait a moment and disappeared back into his house. When he came running back out, he was holding his expensive drone.

"I knew it was a good idea to get the night-vision camera," he said as he set it gently on the snowy ground. He flipped a switch on the bottom and pulled out a controller, motioning his head toward his room. "I'll be able to see above the tree line further than you. If you follow the blinking lights on the drone, I should be able to guide you to where Liam's motorcycle broke down."

Ingenious. I looked at Peter, both impressed and full of gratitude at the same time. "Thanks, Peter. You're a lifesaver."

He nodded at me as he walked back to his room to watch the camera feed. "Let's hope so."

Peter was right. I could even see Delta Road up ahead through a break in the trees. It was a straight shot behind our houses. The problem was getting through the snowy woods in the dark. I pumped my legs as fast as they would carry me, plowing through snow drifts, slipping down icy hills, and scraping my way through branches. I could feel a cut on my face, raw and bleeding a little, but I couldn't stop now. I checked my watch. 8:17. Gritting my teeth, I willed myself to move faster. I knew there couldn't be too much time left.

The drone overhead was easy enough to follow in the pitch black night. It flew at a steady pace, high in the sky, its flashing lights guiding my every step. When it finally stopped and hovered in the sky, I knew I was close. I jumped over a fallen tree and clumsily slid down an embankment toward a dirt road. Here I was finally at Delta Road, the same place where Clark and I had visited before. Or should I say, in the future.

Ahead I heard two distinct voices arguing. I sprinted on the icy road toward them.

There they were. Liam was standing next to a blue truck. His motorcycle was parked in front of a tall evergreen tree. In his hand was a cell phone which he was using to point at the driver as he shouted angrily into the open window. His dark shaggy hair was plastered to his head as the snowflakes fell.

143

Inside the running blue truck, as I had correctly guessed, was Sydney.

"So, you decided that framing me as a drug dealer was the ONLY way to keep me here?" Liam asked furiously, his voice steeped in pain and anger.

"I did it for us! I did it because you couldn't say 'no' to your precious scholarship," Sydney sobbed back through the window, white steam pouring from the tailpipe of the truck. "You know that I didn't get accepted into State. You were still going to go without me! How is that love, Liam? How are we supposed to stay together when we'll be hundreds of miles apart?"

"It's not love," Liam spat back at her, throwing his motorcycle helmet to the side of the road in a rage. "Because you know what, Sydney? I never loved..."

"STOP!" I screamed, nearly wiping out on the treacherously slippery road under my feet as I raced toward them. "Liam, you need to stop right now!"

As I approached them, both Liam and Sydney instantly fell silent and stared at me in confusion. I ran up to Liam and almost slid into him as I came screeching to a halt. I looked down at the ground in wonder. It was insanely icy.

I looked up at Liam and found the words left my mouth. Dark hair touched the tip of his ears. A pair of mystifying hazel eyes stared back at me, trying to place who I was and what I was doing on the side of the road. His tanned skin stood in deep contrast to the white flakes falling around him. Had I not been in a race to save his life, I would've been too smitten to talk to him, let alone start a conversation with him as he was in the middle of breaking up with his beautiful girlfriend.

"Who is she?" Sydney asked in an accusatory voice.

"You don't know me," I answered her, though I kept my eyes on Liam, unable to look away from him. He was still alive. I couldn't believe it. I had to get him off this road if I wanted to keep him alive. "Look, I know this is weird, but you have to trust me. You need to walk away with me, now."

Liam blinked in confusion. He was probably trying to process how I had just appeared out of nowhere in the middle of a snow storm, screaming his name. "What?"

"Listen," I panted. "I know you're hurt. What happened to you with the pills and getting kicked out of the wrestling meet during state qualifications is completely unfair. We can clean this all up, though. The administration doesn't know anything about the drugs found in your locker, so it's not too late to get your scholarship. I know you have a lot of things to say to Sydney right now, but this is definitely not the time. She is in a really bad state."

I wasn't lying there. Sydney's eyes were red and puffy as stains of mascara trailed from her lashes down her cheeks. She looked like she was having a hard time breathing, and she wiped at her running nose unceremoniously with the back of her hand. One hand had a death grip on the steering wheel, her knuckles white. Her hair was frizzy and disheveled. It was hard to picture her as the same girl I had first seen prettily crying about her boyfriend's death. She now seemed hysterical and on the verge of breaking down.

Liam glanced back at me. "You don't get it. She ruined my life!"

I let out a sad laugh. I felt so exhausted I couldn't help myself. "No Liam, trust me. I do get it. I understand everything that happened. Having your best friend and your girlfriend destroy everything you worked so hard for must be devastating. I imagine it feels like the whole world is against you right now."

"How does she know this?" Sydney squealed in outrage.

I held up a finger to hush her and turned back to Liam. "Here's the thing. However awful, misguided, and just plain crazy it was to do what she did—she did it out of love. Maybe a little bit of obsession,

145

too. That same crazy, unpredictable and downright destructive love is still running through her body... I mean, look at her. In the spur of a moment, she took Mike's truck to follow you because she was afraid she'd never see you again."

Liam glanced at the truck. "That's true," he admitted. "She doesn't even know how to drive a stick."

Well, at least I wasn't the only one in this town. I cleared my throat and continued. "I know there are a LOT of things you want to say to her. For now, you need to trust me and walk away."

Shaking his head furiously, Liam gestured angrily toward Sydney. "She needs to know how I feel! You want me to just walk away like nothing ever happened? No, I'm going to let her know exactly what I think about her."

As he started to stomp back toward the truck, I grabbed his arm in sheer frustration. This kid was super stubborn. No wonder he and Nichelle had clashed before. He looked up at me in surprise like he had never been muscled around by a five-foot-two stranger.

"Why, Liam? For what reason? To get the last word? Is that worth your life?" I hissed at him, lowering my voice so that Sydney couldn't hear us.

He jerked his arm away from me. "What are you talking about? I mean, who are you, anyway?"

"Someone who has seen firsthand what angry words can do to someone. I've seen how those little words can bring a whole town to its knees. Trust me Liam, the world is much darker and much colder without you."

His eyebrows went up in surprise as he stared at me. We stood there together in silence for a moment. Liam blinked.

"I've never seen you before, have I?" he asked in a quiet voice.

I shook my head. "No. I just moved here."

"Then why do I have the strangest feeling we've met before?"

I smiled for a moment. We had met before, but trying to explain that to him right now was more than I had the energy for. I held out my hand to him this time, and I knew when he took it, I wouldn't feel an inescapable cold. Liam had his second chance.

"Come on," I said. "Let's take a walk?"

Slowly, Liam nodded at me. "Okay. Hold on, let me just get my things."

As we walked toward the tree where the motorcycle was resting, a wailing rose from inside the truck. Sydney began pounding on the steering wheel and screaming. She struggled for a moment with the stick shift. The engine revved up dangerously on the icy road.

Suddenly, it hit me. I had a much clearer understanding than ever before of what had happened to Liam that night.

"Watch out!" I cried as I pulled Liam into a nearby ditch just as the truck lurched forward, skidded, then crashed into Liam's motorcycle. It pinned the bike against the evergreen. Liam and I landed in the soft snow of the ditch as the branches above us shuddered from the impact, dropping a good six inches of powdered snow on top of us.

Liam shot up, staring at his motorcycle in disbelief. "Oh my god. I could've…" He glanced over at me and offered a hand. "Are you okay?"

I groaned, shaking the snow out of my ears as I searched for my hat. My life seemed destined for frostbite. "Yeah, I'm fine. You?"

He looked at himself as if confirming he were still in one piece. "Yeah. You… you saved my life. She tried to kill me!"

I gazed over at Sydney in the driver's seat of the truck. She was still gripping the steering wheel, knuckles locked, and it looked like she was in complete shock. Her eyes stared straight ahead at nothing as her chest rose up and down rapidly like she was hyperventilating. She choked out a sob. She didn't seem like the calculating malicious killer I had imagined before. She looked scared.

Suddenly, a pair of headlights crested the hill. Up pulled the most disgusting vehicle I had ever seen in my life. I was never more relieved to see the familiar purple eagle across the hood.

"Hey," Clark called from an open window nervously, eyeing me intentionally. "I'm just out for a random snowstorm drive. That's what I do when the roads are treacherously icy, you know. What luck? I'm here to help you now, if you need it."

Clark was obviously the worst at improvisational lying.

He helped Sydney from out of the truck while Liam and I tried to gather ourselves. Shortly after, Sheriff Rankin arrived, fortunately called in quickly by a concerned citizen who I later found out was Nichelle. She had also raced to the school and confirmed that Mike's truck was missing, Mike himself was still at the wrestling meet and oblivious to the fact that his keys and truck were gone.

"So, who the hell are you, and what do you have to do with all this?" Sheriff Rankin asked suspiciously as I sat in the back of his squad car with a blanket wrapped around me.

I had to take a moment to remember we were back in the past. He didn't know me yet. I suppose wandering around on a dirt road in the middle of the night did seem a bit odd.

"Let me make this easy for you," I said. I glanced around to make sure we were out of earshot from the others. "I'm Toki Tooley. My grandmother is Emi Murakami. You and I have already met. You called me a 'pissant', just so you know. It was completely unprovoked."

The hardness in his eyes softened. He looked almost relieved to see me, which was a first.

"Another Protector, huh?" he asked, lowering his voice. "That kid, Liam, he was…"

I nodded.

The sheriff whistled, looking to the steaming blue truck still stuck against the tree. "All right, what happened?"

"Sydney doesn't know how to drive a stick shift that well, and the roads are insanely icy. I think she accidentally put it in the wrong gear when she tried to go in reverse, and the truck jumped forward. They had just broken up. She wasn't thinking straight."

"You're tellin' me, if you weren't there to get him out of the way, then she would've killed him?"

I didn't answer.

Rankin nodded slowly for a moment, piecing together all of the information. "Hmmm. Drivin' a stolen vehicle, reckless drivin'. Should I also add attempted murder to that list?"

He and I made meaningful eye contact. Suddenly, everything my grandmother had told me before was starting to make sense.

Their future is not your future. Second chances only are given to all who accept them.

"Their" future. Second chances only are given to "all." The ramblings of Grandmother's journal made so much sense now. It had tried to tell me all along this just wasn't about one person. By solving the crime, I was able to return to the past to stop my future from happening. In my future, Sydney had accidentally killed Liam and covered up the crime. But that wasn't the future anymore now that he was alive. I wasn't just saving Liam from his untimely death. I was also saving Sydney from making a horrible mistake that would follow her around for the rest of her life. Both she and Liam now had a second chance to live their lives differently.

What had happened to Liam in my future was a tragic, completely avoidable accident, but it still was an accident.

"Not attempted murder. Just terrible judgement and probably some daddy issues," I told the sheriff.

"You sure? You know the best out of all of us."

I glanced at Sydney who was sitting in another patrol car. She looked completely deflated and miserable. She chewed on her fingernails morosely.

"Yeah. I'm certain."

"Great. Good work, kid. Looks like you really are your grandmother's kin. Now what else do I need to know about this would-be crime?"

I told him everything that had happened; Mike and Sydney's plan to frame Liam and keep him out of state for wrestling, the cover-up of his death, Coach Rossi's drinking demons and subsequent blackmailing, and the illicit pill market at Chamberlain High.

"Charming. Sounds like I'm going to have myself a busy week," Sheriff Rankin sighed. He reached out and shook my hand roughly. "Well, Toki Tooley, it's been nice to meet you. I'm sure you and I will have many more heartwarming experiences together. Now, if you excuse me..."

I scooted forward in the seat hastily. "Wait a minute. You owe me."

Rankin glanced at me, annoyed. "Excuse me?"

"You... well, future you, told me that if I solved the murder, you'd go to the principal of the high school and tell him what an amazing person I am."

He blinked at me and let out a string of curses which I wanted to point out I had heard before.

"You gotta be kiddin' me. You think I have time to do this?"

I crossed my arms firmly. "You promised."

"Ugh. Fine. Whaddya' want me to say?"

I told him exactly what he should say to the principal and made him repeat it three times. Finally, I was satisfied he remembered everything.

"You have to tell him Monday morning," I reminded him. "Um, please."

He groaned as he tilted his hat over his eyes. "Okay, kid, whatever. Don't expect me to do this every time, okay? Ugh, darn millennials think the world owes them a favor every time they stop a murder. Now, if you excuse me, I've got to drive Mr. Hot-Shot over there home to his parents and explain why his motorcycle looks like a heap of scrap metal."

Off he went, grumbling about today's youth, their clothes, skateboarding, and whatever else old people generally decide to complain about.

Clark came sauntering up to me casually, running a hand through his tousled hair. 'Uh excuse me, miss, but I couldn't help notice that you might need a ride home. Your chariot awaits."

"Clark, don't you think one near death experience for me tonight is enough?"

"You know, Toki, technically we haven't met yet. You aren't aware of how horribly dangerous my van is. Really, you should be giving me a first chance. Otherwise, that's just being super judgey."

There was a logic to his thinking. I nodded. "Okay."

As we walked to his van, he said, "Anyway, I was thinking that tomorrow I can pick you up in the morning and we can go to school together."

I shook my head. "No, Clark. Like you just said, we haven't met yet. I'm not enrolled in school until Monday. I have to unpack my whole house—again."

Facing me sadly, he tilted his head like a puppy. "What? You mean I don't get to meet you until Monday? Gah. This whole-time traveling thing is really screwing with my brain."

"Well on the upside, maybe now you have some time to think of a proper way to introduce yourself instead of, you know, stalking me in the halls."

He brightened at the thought. "Ooooh. Good point. I'll put my best thinking cap on for this one!"

As Clark struggled with opening the passenger door for me, I took a quick glance back at Liam. He looked shaken, but he was alive. I felt a huge weight lift off of me. He looked up at me, and we stared at each other for a moment. I smiled and waved awkwardly, then turned and climbed into the van.

*Sunday, February 7th. 4:29 p.*m.

THIS TIME, THE VISIT with Grandmother was dramatically different. When we came in, she was wide awake. She and my mother and father chatted sunnily with each other, and though there were some awkward pauses and that familiar far-off look in Mom's eyes, everything felt so much better than the first visit.

I wanted desperately to talk to Grandmother about what had happened. Did she have the journal? Did she know what I had done? I couldn't help but notice the clock sitting by Grandmother's bedside, ticking away brightly. I gave it a small smile, knowing exactly what it would say to me if I tried to talk to it. I sat by quietly as my family visited, wishing for another miracle to come my way.

Apparently, miracles do come true, even twice, in Devil's Ford. Near the end of our visit, there was a knock on the door, and a familiar-looking face popped in.

"Uh, excuse me, Mr. and Mrs. Tooley?" Sheriff Rankin asked my parents, pointedly ignoring me. "I was wondering if I could have a word with you two in private?"

As my parents stepped in the hallway, Rankin winked at me. "Five minutes, kid," he said in a low voice as he closed the door.

"You did it, Toki!" Grandmother exclaimed, pulling the journal out from under her pillow and showing me the page with Liam's murder. Sure enough, there was a shimmering stamp at the end of the entry. I frowned at the page, confused.

"I know I wrote Sydney's name at the bottom of the page. Where did it go?"

Grandmother smiled gently at me. "Surely you know by now?"

I thought about it for a moment then groaned at my own thick-headedness. Of course! Second chances. Liam and Sydney both had their second chance. If she never committed the crime, she wasn't guilty of anything. That explained why there were no other guilty names, only the shimmering mark.

She handed me the journal. "This is yours now. I'm afraid you may have to sign it again; it can be a stickler for the rules. You are now the Protector of this town. You have to keep us all safe from the influence of the Dark Spirit. It's a heavy burden, dear one, but without you, there would be no hope for Devil's Ford."

I took the journal in my hands and stared at it for a moment. "Grandmother, I have a question about the Dark Spirit. I recognized it when I tried to talk to it. It was Liam, wasn't it?"

She looked sadly at me. "Yes, it was. When people are killed here, Toki, their spirit lingers. It grows angry, it grows sad, and it demands to be avenged and recognized. It cannot rest easy in this town for whatever reason. Without Protectors, this whole town would be overrun by spirits who refuse to leave. You help everyone—the guilty, the innocent—come back to the light. The Protectors restore the light to a dark and cold world."

"If the Dark Spirit was Liam, what does that make the Light Spirit? I thought Sheriff Rankin said I had to defeat the Dark Spirit."

"Foster always thinks about things in black and white, dear Toki. I remind him frequently that although black and white are easy to see, most of the things around us are shades of color. Putting things into categories of 'good' and 'evil' negates many of the unique qualities of the spirits of this world. He sees the Dark Spirit as evil, as though it were something that must be stopped. You may think of it more as a misguided spirit, something that needs calming, nurturing, and care."

"So, the Light Spirit is…"

Grandmother gestured to me. "It is the Protectors of the town. You and all the past Protectors have a spirit so bright that you can guide any darkness back home. Your spirit and their spirits are all bound to the journal. Knowledge on guiding the darkness to the light has been passed down in that journal. It will never run out of pages, not until the final darkness turns to the light."

I thought about my interactions with the Dark Spirit. Grandmother was right. Although it felt deathly cold and lonely, there was no malice. It felt lost, like a grieving shadow. Thinking about the Dark Spirits that way made me feel a little better. Evil spirits were still just things of fairy tales. Protectors dealt with lost spirits.

"I think Liam remembered me from when he was a Dark Spirit," I admitted. "Is that going to be a problem?"

Grandmother Emi laughed, making my anxieties melt away. "Oh no. There's always some glimmer of recognition from the lost when you save them, particularly from those with strong spirits. You'll find they'll help you in ways that you'd never expect later on."

There were so many questions I wanted to ask Grandmother about being a Protector, but I knew my time was running short. I had to get something off my chest before my parents came back.

"Grandmother, I know there's been some... issues between mom and you."

Her face grew so grim I almost regretted asking it. "Yes. All of that is my fault. I forgot the second rule of the journal when I was raising your mother, and it pushed her away. Then, when your Grandfather died, it was the final nail in the coffin. I lost my way for a long time."

"Their future is not your future," I recalled aloud. I stopped, the realization slowly dawning on me. "You mean Mom was..."

Grandmother confirmed with a short nod of her head. "Yes. She was killed when she was just a teenager. Fortunately, I was able to bring her spirit back. However, when her father was killed a few years later, I was overwhelmed. I ran out of time, and he never got a second chance.

To this day, he is still a Dark Spirit, out there somewhere. Both of those experiences scarred me for life, and I'm afraid your mother bore the brunt of that pain." She took a deep shaky breath. "As I may have said before, child, being a Protector is a burden. Failure weighs heavily on your heart and changes who you are. It can destroy your relationships and push those you love the most far away from you. I am so sorry to have asked this of you."

I wanted to ask her more. How did my Grandfather die? How did she manage to give my mother a second chance? Unfortunately, at that moment, Mom and Dad walked back in. I looked at my Grandmother with questioning eyes. She smiled at me, as if to say *There will be time later.*

"Here, child," she said to me as we got ready to leave. "I want you to have this. It's a family heirloom, and it will look better in your home than in this little room."

She handed me the clock. My parents regarded me with confused looks as I grinned down at it, holding it carefully in my arms.

Important, we both thought together.

Chapter Fifteen: DéjàVu

Monday, February 8th. 7:35 a.m.

M Y (second) FIRST DAY of school was remarkably different than my first first day. Mom pulled up into the drop-off lane in front of the school and smiled at me.

"You know, you're adjusting far better than I thought you would. I was worried you'd be a nervous wreck today, but you almost seem like you've done this before."

I smiled quietly to myself. Oh, how right you are, Mom.

"I have a good feeling about this place," I told her. "Thanks for moving us here. I know I wasn't excited at first, but I think it's a good change for me, you know?"

She gave me a look. "Promise not to tell the kids what the plungers are saying?"

"No plungers this time," I promised. I couldn't imagine that a plunger would have anything useful to say about future murders, so I figured I could at least keep that vow.

Smiling warmly at me, my mom gave me a kiss on the forehead and waved for way too long as I hopped out of the car and walked up the steps of Chamberlain High School.

As I approached the main office, there was a law enforcement officer waiting for me, tapping his shoe impatiently and regarding me with a look that I knew was going to be the first of many. Luckily, he wasn't there to arrest me. Not today, anyway.

"Well, pipsqueak," Sheriff Rankin said as I walked up, "nice of you to finally show up."

"You too. I know I'm taking you away from all your busy campaigning against all those political rivals that want to take your spot as sheriff… oh wait. Right. You've run unopposed for basically forever. This should be no skin off your back."

He grumbled as he opened the door to the main office and motioned me to follow him. As we waited to meet with the principal, he glanced at me.

"Your grandmother said you did good, kid. Keep it up."

We had quite a story to tell the principal about saving Liam's life. There was so much to share about what happened, but we had to be careful to explain it in a way that made sense since technically the investigation had never happened. Some of it was true, some of it was loosely based off real events, and other parts were completely fabricated. I had to give the old guy credit, Sheriff Rankin could spin a story well. There were times I leaned forward to listen to him speak, fascinated by how easily he could explain events that never happened. I guess he had a lot of practice doing this with Grandmother Emi. The two seemed like they had shared a lot of adventures together, so he had to be a pro at this by now. For the most part, I just leaned back and told my (carefully rehearsed) part of the tale. Sheriff Rankin took a lot of credit for the things I had discovered, like the prescription pills and Rossi's drinking. I didn't mind. Truthfully, the more removed from it all that I could be, the better.

It was lunchtime by the time we finished up our story. I was then excused with my swag bag full of Hive Days gear. As I left, I could hear the principal and the Sheriff begin discussing the finer legal details of the Rossi, Mike, and Sydney investigation. I followed a glowing Mrs. Fieldman down to the cafeteria as she gave me a quick tour with unbridled enthusiasm.

"I apologize that we didn't have time for you to get to your morning classes, but you seem like the kind of student that will jump right into things! Follow me over to the Buzzers table; I need to check in with them very quickly."

There they were, my three friends. All were sitting at the detention table. Nichelle, Clark, and Peter stared at me with the same knowing looks on their faces that told me they all remembered.

"Buzzers!" Mrs. Fieldman sang in a voice that made my eardrums vibrate. "I've got some good news for you! Seems like a Best Buzzer has already been chosen!"

All three captives glanced at each other in confusion.

Mrs. Fieldman pointed to me dramatically and continued. "This new student here, Toki Tooley, has told me that one of you fearlessly led her through the woods when she got lost last week. Toki came to our office and told us all about it even before knowing about the Best Buzzer competition. Peter Li, congratulations on being awarded Best Buzzer! You are now free to depart the detention table."

Stunned, Peter threw a questioning look to me as he picked up his lunch tray and left the table. I thought I saw a hint of a smile on his face as he left.

"You two," Mrs. Fieldman continued, directing her full attention on to Clark and Nichelle, "the sheriff stopped by this morning and told me that you have been volunteering your time to help your community. He said you were upstanding role models of what young people could do to help others in times of need. He also went on to say he has never seen a young woman and young man of your caliber in this town before. I think he even mentioned you two being in running for 'Citizens of the Year'. What an honor!"

I grinned to myself. Apparently making the Sheriff repeat his speech three times had worked. He had included every minute detail I told him to say, whether it was true or not.

Mrs. Fieldman beamed appraisingly at Nichelle and Clark. "This is exactly the kind of behavior I'd expect out of my Buzzers. You two are also excused from the detention table."

Clark let out a whoop that echoed around the lunchroom and cartwheeled clumsily off in a different direction. Nichelle pumped her fist and jumped up. She grabbed her tray and walked away with a proud smile.

Mrs. Fieldman gave me a large smile. "Well, welcome to Chamberlain High, Toki! Have a 'buzz' worthy first day!"

As she pranced away, I sat down at the Buzzers' table which was now completely empty. Great, I thought to myself. My first act of kindness may have actually lost me the only friends I had. I pulled out a pear from my sack lunch and stared at it moodily when a tray slid in next to me.

"Sorry, just had to get my lunch," Clark said, already chewing food with an open mouth. "It's weird that somehow, you can sit in a place for a couple of months and feel like you're stuck there. You never really realize how beautiful your view is." He winked at me. "Clark Kent. Nice to meet you. Was… that better than the first time?"

I smiled at him. "Much better. Maybe next time let's work on not lying about your name, okay?"

"Good luck with that," a snort responded. "By the way, Clark, we're not Buzzers anymore. You can lay off the flirting." Nichelle sat across from me with her tray. "But I get what you're saying. Sitting at the same place for so long… it would just feel weird to sit anywhere else in the cafeteria, you know?"

Without a word, Peter also returned, slipping back into the other side of the table, though maybe a little bit closer than he was before.

"Peter, you're back!" Clark rejoiced. "Did you miss me?"

He was immediately flipped off.

"Aww, I missed you too, buddy," Clark responded brightly.

I stared at the three of them in disbelief. "Let me get this straight. I just spent my one favor from the sheriff getting you guys all out of detention, and you're going to STAY at this table willingly?"

"Well, yes," Nichelle said, frowning. "I mean, it was awesome of you to get us all out of detention. Pretty smart thinking, actually. All the other tables are full, though. Can't have anybody eavesdropping on your little secret, can we? Talking to the spirits and solving murders isn't really something that these other fools would understand. We're much more accepting than they are."

Peter nodded. "We can help you. We want to help you."

Clark agreed enthusiastically, shoveling food into his mouth at an alarming rate. "That's right! We're a team, now. Between your 'spirit communication', Nichelle's fists, Peter's brains, and my stunning good looks, we can solve anything. So, what's the next case?"

I shrugged as I pulled out Grandmother's journal from my pocket. I had signed the back page last night, binding myself to the journal for the second time. My wrists once again had a faint trace of white light proving that I now was the Protector of the town. The clock had ticked quietly and comfortably all night long. For the first time in a week, I got a peaceful and deep sleep.

As I laid the book on the table, my eyes caught sight of Liam, sitting at a lunch table surrounded by a sea of friends. He looked oddly apart from all of them and kept his head down as if in deep thought. He looked up, and his eyes caught mine. He stared at me with a look I couldn't quite place.

Nichelle noticed too and raised her eyebrows. "Whoa. Looks like you made another friend. Or... enemy?"

I glanced away from him, embarrassed and unsure of myself.

Maybe rushing into the scene without any explanation had saved him in time, but it probably had really rattled him, too. I was supposed to be a 'new kid', and I knew all about his most personal, painful details. I made a note that next time, I should probably try to play it a little more smoothly.

Grandmother had told me that the 'lost' would help me in ways I never would expect. I wondered how Liam would repay me one day, and if I could ever convince him that I was just a normal teenage girl.

"I think everything is safe for now," I said. "Hopefully my life is more than just solving murders. Maybe I'll finally have time to settle in and learn how to find my classes in this maze."

Peter spoke up. "Hey, do you guys want to come over to my house on Friday? We're having dumplings... again." He looked slightly nauseous at the thought.

He didn't have to invite any of us twice. The thought of double dumplings just added to the perks of being a Protector. It seemed like there could be some real benefits from getting to live your life over twice. With any luck, Nichelle, Clark, Peter and I would make sure that the people in Devil's Ford got their second chance, too.

Murder at the Mountain Trails
A Toki Tooley Mystery Series

The mystery continues . . .

Monday, February 22nd. 10:03 a.m.

If you happen to be unlucky enough to listen to all the inanimate spirits in the world, the one vehicle you don't want to be stuck in a conversation with is a school bus. They are by far the most miserable and depressing automobile spirits out there. They also tend to be the most talkative (three words, every time!) and over-share about their daily experiences to anyone foolish enough to ask.

I tried everything to avoid communicating with that old bus as we wound our way up the narrow trek to Mountain Trails. I kept my hands in my pockets, I tried reading, and I even tried to engage in conversation with my three friends who had goaded me to go on this trip in the first place. That didn't work. Apparently Nichelle's early morning training session and cutting criticism of my self-defense skills had left her exhausted. Through some sort of miracle, she had fallen asleep on the way up and was dozing through every teeth-rattling pothole we hit.

Peter was playing some game on his phone, and from the intense look on his face, it was best not to disturb him. Every now and then he would look up in unbridled gamer annoyance at the front of the bus where some tiny freshman was grinning back at him and waving.

165

It was safe to assume that Peter had met his match in his online game, but he didn't seem to be going down without a fight.

Clark had sequestered himself at the very back of the bus, hood drawn over his head as he sat against the window and plucked at his guitar strings. He was probably still mad at me. Every now and then he would pause, scribbling down music notes on a sheet of paper, then beam proudly at his work. I didn't have the heart to tell him that despite our earlier disagreement, he was still only using three guitar chords in the whole song.

I sighed and tried to look out the window at the passing trees. Grandmother's ugly scarf that she had so painstakingly knitted for me was still bunched up in a huge ball in the pocket of my winter jacket. I couldn't imagine a time I would willingly put it on, but if I ever needed a jump rope, I was ready to go.

I was out of options at this point and figured we still had plenty of time left in our ascent up the mountain. Bored out of my mind, I was about to reach my hand out to touch the cool metal side of the bus when *he* slid into the seat in front of me. Dark brown shaggy hair. Awful yellow and black athletic jacket. Soul-searching hazel eyes.

"Hey," Liam said, ignoring the bus driver's warnings to stay seated at all times.

Ever since I had miraculously intervened and saved him from a distraught girlfriend with a lead foot and a stolen truck, Liam seemed to always be watching me warily from a distance. I guess I couldn't blame him. If a random person that I never met before had appeared out of the woods and saved me from certain death, I probably would be a little suspicious too. Sheriff Rankin had warned me to keep a lower profile in the future, and I saw why. Liam was looking at me as if I had a wild tiger hidden behind me that was ready to pounce. Thank goodness he hadn't caught me in the act of having a conversation with the bus. That would've been hard to explain.

"Hi," I squeaked back pathetically. Focus, Tooley, I told myself. You've already made yourself stand out, so for once try to act like you don't care about the innermost thoughts of a hair dryer.

Unfortunately, blending in was easier said than done. Staring at my face, Liam squinted in the glare of the light filtering through the grimy window. "Your eye. Did you get into a fight or something?" he asked.

I put my hand up to my face which still felt tender to the touch. I knew I was going to get a black eye. Thanks a lot, Nichelle.

"Um, I do a little light kickboxing before school. Helps me control my deep inner rage, you know?" I joked weakly.

Liam looked unconvinced. "Uh-huh. Do you always make a habit out of saving people, or was it just me?"

I shook my head so furiously I thought my brain would be spinning for days. "Um no, it's not a habit. I don't save people all the time. It was just you. I mean, not that you're special or anything." My heart dropped when I saw the look on his face. "Oh well, you. I mean, YOU are special. Just not to me."

My brain finally recuperated enough to tell my mouth it would be a good time to shut up. I shakily grabbed my water bottle and took a drink, hoping it would buy me some time to think of a response that didn't sound like I was a blithering idiot.

He frowned for a moment, then chose wisely to move on. "Right. So, anyway, you ready to go talk to some trees?"

What!? Did he know about my ability to talk to spirits? In surprise I gasped at his question. Unfortunately, water and airways don't mix well. I immediately spit out all the water I was drinking across the aisle which earned me a very special glare from Peter as he wiped off his phone like I had spewed the plague on it. Through my gagging and choking, I tried desperately to think of what it was that had given me away. Had I talked to something too carelessly? Did Liam see that one tense disagreement I had with a lunch tray one day? Would the rest of the school know, too?

"Talk to trees?" I gasped between coughs at a bewildered-looking Liam. "Why would I do that?"

Liam shrugged as he looked at me, probably half-wondering if he should try to help me through my choking spell.

"I don't know. That's what they have us do up here for 'quiet time'. Talk to trees, count pinecones, take in the beauty of nature. You know, all that eco-planet new age stuff. I mean, I guess this is your first time up here, so it's all going to be new and kinda weird. Just wanted to give you a heads-up."

I finally was able to catch my breath. "Oh. Yeah. New age stuff. Well, I guess don't be surprised if you see me talking to a rock then, right?"

Liam grinned at me like maybe I wasn't the biggest spaz on the planet, then nodded and waved at me awkwardly. He went back to his old seat despite the empty threats from the bus driver. I wanted to bury myself into the seat cushions and never come out. Why was I so on edge about this trip?

I thought quietly for a moment but couldn't resist myself. Sitting all alone and trying to contain my anxiety was making me a nervous wreck. I needed an outlet; I had to talk to the bus. Surely it was having a more terrible time on this trek up the mountain than I was. Hearing the familiar grumblings of the school bus would at least let me know that all was still right with the world.

I wasn't prepared for the answer I received, and it put me in an even worse mood than before.

Beware, was all the bus said.

CPSIA information can be obtained
at www.ICGtesting.com
Printed in the USA
BVHW042112080820
585911BV00012B/554